DEATH
OF A
SECRET

CHRISTY MANN

DEATH
OF A
SECRET

CHRISTY MANN

Death of a Secret
Christy Mann
@2018 Christy Mann

For rights, bulk publishing, and other publication information or to report errors, send letter to:
Publisher – Twisted Souls Press
PO Box 569
Roy, Utah 84067

Cover design by Fantasia Covers, http://www.fantasiacover-design.com/

To the Best Fans on the Planet!

You are what feeds my drive to keep going as a writer. I would have given up a long time ago on this writing thing if it were not for you. You are what keeps pushing me forward, improving, and bringing better and better stories out of my head and into your hands. I appreciate you more than I will ever be able to convey in a few short words.

Your reviews matter, your emails and messages matter. Keep them coming! I love you!

Chapter 1

Sarah is lining up her shot on the 8 ball. It's a tricky bank shot and Sarah hates them. Playing as often as she does with her friends, she knows she can make the shot. She ends up scratching, costing her and her teammate the game. Failing herself and her teammate Nate. It breaks her a little inside.

It's just a game. She knows this and knows that the razzing she gets from her friends afterward is just harmless teasing. But to her, making this particular shot has been a challenge too long now, it's one she aims to conquer.

This time, she concentrates. Shutting out the shit talking from the opposing team, Sophie and Todd, and fighting the butterflies she gets from Nate staring at her the way he does. She takes a deep breath and closes her eyes. She opens them, pulls back on the cue, and pushes it forward, connecting with the solid white ball on the table. She watches, unable to move, as the cue ball taps the solid black ball with a loud crack. The eight ball rolls right toward its intended target. It falls.

Everyone holds their breath now. The tension is palpable. They are all hesitant to cheer, just yet. The cue ball comes back and is heading right for the corner pocket. Nate yells at it to stop when it hits the halfway mark on the table. It refuses his request.

Sophie's hands squeeze tightly into Todd's shoulder as the ball continues to roll. almost in slow motion. Todd whispers a silent prayer. Sarah is frozen in place. The whole world seems to have stopped, except for the solid white ball. She holds her breath.

It stops. A hair's breadth from the edge of the pocket, it sits. Cheers erupt from Nate and Sarah. Boos and hisses come from Todd. Sophie stumbles around, clenching her midsection like she has been struck and is in the final throes of her life.

Sarah stands upright and exhales. Her bottom lip juts out and she blows a long strand of strawberry blonde hair away from her sweat soaked face. Overwhelmed by relief and pride, she can't fight the flush of blood flowing into her cheeks or the smile that stretches across her mouth. She turns to high five Nate. He ignores her raised hand and wraps her in a hug. He plants little kisses on her forehead.

Her soul sister, Sophie, jokingly tells her that she cheated and needs to take the shot again. Sarah gives her the middle finger over Nate's shoulder. She hesitantly pulls herself out of Nate's embrace and walks toward Sophie and Todd. Todd high fives her while Sophie smacks her on the ass. Sarah jumps and winces like Sophie has wounded her. They all tell her good job and Sophie hands her a mug of warm draft beer like it's a trophy.

Sarah laughs and takes the mug. She bows slightly to everyone and raises her trophy so the crowd can see it. No one else is paying attention. She shrugs and takes a long slog of the bitter ale. Her nose wrinkles and her eyes squint as the bite and the warmth fill her mouth. She spits the liquid back into the cup and slams it down on the table. 'Oh my god that's gross!' Everyone nods in agreement. 'I should probably do something about that.'

It's the end of the night and the crowd has dwindled by about half when Sophie looks at Sarah and winks. 'It's time to shut it down love.'

'Awww, do we gotta?' Sarah whines jokingly. Since she and Sophie own the place, it's their job to run the rest of the crowd off. Sarah doesn't really look forward to closing time. There is usually at least one drunk guy or girl that refuses to leave, and Sophie deals with it. Sometimes the cops get called. Tonight, things seem peaceful.

Sarah kisses Nate on the top of the head as she walks off to start collecting glasses around the room. She carries seven of them to the bar and sets them on the counter. The bartender, Jared, winks at her from the sink. She nods at him. There is a bucket full of fresh soapy water and bar towels sitting on the counter waiting for her.

Before she grabs the bucket to start cleaning tables, she pulls out her phone and contemplates calling her dad. He would be proud of her winning moment. He taught her to play after all. Her screen lit up with the date and time. It was late already. He would be on his way to bed if not there already. She decided to tell him about it in person in the morning.

Sarah tucked her phone back into her pocket and grabbed the bucket and turned around. She nearly ran smack dab into Nate's chest face first. He caught her by her arms. The bucket squished between them for a second. The water sloshed and spilled over its brim, soaking Nate straight down his front. Sarah brought her hands up to her mouth and she gasped. Nate grabbed the bucket with both hands the instant Sarah let go, saving it from becoming a puddle of wet soapiness on the floor.

'Oh god honey, I'm so sorry!' Her hands were still covering her wide-open mouth.

Nate turned and set the bucket down on the table next to him. He turned back toward her and looked down at his clothes. He looked back up at her. She was staring at him, wide eyed. He shrugged. 'It's just a little water babe. No big deal.'

She nodded her head as she stared at him. She ran her finger along the buttons of his soaked shirt. It was clinging to him in the nicest way. 'It should have been a bigger bucket.' She winked at him. Man, she loved this guy.

She turned to grab a towel from the bucket, and he reached for her. She squealed as he stuck his belly out toward her and growled like a monster. She plunged her hands into the bucket and flung water out of it at him. They were both wet and laughing when Sophie came out of the back somewhere and yelled at them to get a room.

Sarah and Nate both reached into the bucket and pulled out towels. They wrung them out and lobbed them at Sophie. She didn't miss a lick. She caught one and then the other in one fail swoop, still holding on to a broom in the other hand. 'Nice try!' She laughed and walked toward Todd. She tossed him a bar towel and they all got to work. It would take all four of them a solid two hours to get the place cleaned and ready for the next day.

Sarah loved these nights. Even though it was a lot of work, doing it with her best friend and Todd and Nate here helping, it was worth it. She loved this place.

Chapter 2

Sarah was about as relaxed as a person could be. Floating around in the pool at midday in early summer. Her thoughts fluttered between work and Nate, her chores were done and she didn't have a care in the world until early evening. Life was good.

Her epic win the night before flashed through her mind. She hadn't seen her dad yet, so she hadn't even told him the news. He would be so proud of her and she couldn't wait to tell him.

She flipped over off of the raft keeping her afloat and raced out of the pool. She grabbed her towel and wrapped it around herself and headed toward the house. Her mother would kill her for dripping through the house. She stopped on the stoop and dried herself off a bit.

When she was confident she wouldn't drip all over the place, she draped the towel over the railing and went inside.

When she reached the small hall outside the study, she stopped dead in her tracks. She heard her dad talking with someone so she crept up to the door and crouched to watch the interaction without interrupting.

JACOB STOOD up and walked around his desk. He stopped directly in front of a man Sarah didn't recognize. He gestured for him to stand up. He said, 'I am sorry there isn't more I can do for you in this matter Mr. Murphy. If there's nothing else?'

The man shot to his feet. 'Oh, but there is Mr. Rosenthal. I know something, and it is going to cost you seventy-five thousand dollars to keep me quiet. Cash.' He spit the last word out with as much confidence as he could muster.

Sarah watched Latham lean forward in his seat, ready to intervene if need be. Jacob sat back on his desk and scratched his head. He shook his head at Latham and gestured for him to stand down. Latham leaned back and relaxed.

'Seventy-five thousand dollars, cash? For what? This better be damn good.' Jacob couldn't contain his chuckle.

'An affair.' The man just threw it out there.

Jacob almost rolled off of his desk laughing. 'I've never had an affair.'

'Olivia has. With me. It's been a while, but...'

The laughing stopped. Jacob's head snapped forward and he glared at the man sitting in front of him. 'Olivia? Bullshit! When?'

'About twenty years ago. When she came and told me she was pregnant, I cut if off. I had a wife and a three-year-old son to worry about. So, I sent her on her way. I quit my job at the bank and got hired at the Senator's office the next day. I was living happily ever after until you cut me off at the knees.'

He nodded and stood there with his arms crossed, waiting.

'Twenty years ago? She told you she was pregnant?' Jacob's eyes squinted.

'Yes, sir. I figured you were well off and could handle it or would make her have an abortion. I really didn't give a shit. I had my own family to think about. So, I told her to go home. She has it good here, does she not, and the girl, she's fine here, right?'

The look of confidence on the man's face faltered for a moment as Jacob peered into him. The veins in Jacob's forehead throbbed and his nostrils flared. He reached up and grabbed the man by his throat with both hands.

In a moment, the man's body went limp.

Latham jumped to his feet. 'Sir!'

Jacob let go of the man's neck as if he expected him to stand on his feet and adjust his tie. Instead, he collapsed to the floor like a bowl of overcooked pasta. As he fell, his body twisted to the side and his neck bent over the arm of the chair with a loud crack. Then he slithered the rest of the way to the floor.

Latham and Jacob stood there, exchanging a glance. Latham finally rushed to the stranger's side and leaned his ear next to the man's mouth. 'He isn't breathing sir.'

Jacob's eyes were glassy. He ran his hand over his mouth and turned to his left. He walked around his desk and sank back in his chair. His chest heaved with each breath.

'Get him out of here!' Jacob bellowed at Latham.

'Shouldn't we call 911 sir, or perform some CPR or something?' Latham made no attempt to save the man's life.

'No. Do away with him, somewhere he will never be found. Scum like him...' Jacob's voice trailed off.

'Yes, sir. Right away.'

'Come back to see me when it is finished. I will pay you well if this goes away and I never hear about it again.' He buried his face in his hands.

'Yes, sir.'

Latham gathered the limp body in his arms and hoisted him up over his shoulder. 'Is there somewhere I can get something to wrap him in? I shouldn't just stroll out with a body on my shoulder.'

'Guest house. Pull around to the back.'

Jacob opened up the drawer to his left and pulled out a key ring. 'The gold is to the gate, the silver to the door.' He tossed them to Latham.

Latham caught the keys in midair, slid them into his shirt pocket and headed toward the door.

SO MANY THOUGHTS bombard Sarah's brain. Her mom having an affair and getting pregnant wasn't so far fetched. The idea that she she could have had a brother or sister was her first thought and it made her a little angry. Then it hit her. Twenty-one years ago. That baby would have been her.

The connections were being made in her brain at break neck speed, but it seemed like slow motion to Sarah. The man in Latham's arms, the man her father just choked to death, is her father? He had a son at the time, so she could have a brother, but now he is dead and she will never know for sure. She needed to sit down. She backed up a few steps and plopped down on the stairs.

Chapter 3

Latham carried the body into the hallway, turned and closed the study door behind him. When he turned back around, he saw Sarah sitting on the stairs. Her eyes were about as glossy as Jacob's. She stared straight ahead and slowly turned her head back and forth, muttering something incoherent.

'How much of that did you catch?' Latham asked her.

She didn't respond.

Latham stepped toward her and snapped his fingers in front of her face. She jumped and glared up at him. Not sure how long he had been there.

'What?' she asked, confused.

'How long have you been sitting here?'

'Oh, ummm, just long enough to see what happened to him. I just wanted to come tell dad something epic. I can't remember what it was now though.'

Thoughts swirled in her head and made her feel dizzy and ill.

Latham leaned over and grabbed her by her arm. Yanking her to her feet, she stood up and he led her by her arm in front of him out the back door. They followed the sidewalk to the guest house that was nestled between two trees out against the back wall. When they reached the door of the small cottage, he forcefully shoved Sarah in front of him and told her to open the door.

Sarah turned and looked at him. 'I have to go inside and get my keys.'

Latham pulled out the keys Jacob had given him and threw them to her. She made no attempt to catch them. He shifted the heft of the body on his shoulder ensuring he didn't lose his hold. 'Now. Open it.'

Sarah bent over and picked the keys up. Her hands shook as she slid the silver key into the lock and turned the knob. She just wanted to go up to her room and think. She stepped to the side so he could go in and leave him to whatever he was going to do now.

Instead, before she could turn and walk away, he grabbed her by the arm again and shoved her inside ahead of him. He kicked the door closed behind him. He looked around the room. The living area may have been small, but it held a small love seat and that was where he set the body down. He looked around again.

Sarah turned and tried to pull away from Latham and leave. He tightened his grip on her for a moment, positioning her in front of the chair, and then shoved her toward it. 'Sit!' he barked at her.

She flopped backwards into the plush upholstery of the chair so hard that the wooden legs slid a few inches across the tile floor. It tilted ever so slightly onto just the back legs and then settled with a crack. She crossed her arms and pulled her feet up into the chair under her.

Latham eyed her up and down, trying to ignore the thoughts about her racing in his mind and creating a stir in his pants. He looked away from her and back to the issue at hand. The man lying on the couch. He had some time, he thought, but not much. He yelled at her over his shoulder. 'Bring me two sheets.

Sarah just sat there. She was trying to get her head wrapped around what had happened. Seeing the man lying there on the couch should have solidified it for her, but somehow, it didn't. She had so many questions, and wanted answers, but was sure she wouldn't like what they were. She didn't even hear Latham's question at first.

'Did you not hear me? Bring me some sheets, now!' He barked at her again. Her whole body jostled as his voice boomed through the tiled room.

She jumped to her feet, the numbness in them causing her to stumble slightly as she thudded on bare feet into the closet in the bedroom. She had no idea what it was he wanted from her. She stood there for a solid minute, trying to recall his demand.

When she couldn't for the life of her remember, she tiptoed back to the doorway leading into the living room. She poked her head back out of the bedroom door and asked, 'What did you want again?'

The frustration in his sigh was palpable and made her aware of the seriousness of the situation. She really didn't remember, though. She stood there, with just her head poking out of the doorway, waiting for his answer. She didn't like the way he looked at her. It was frustration, mixed with something that made her skin crawl. She didn't like him. She never had. This was not endearing him to her any either.

'Sheets! Come on Sarah, I need to wrap him up so I can carry him out of here. Bring me two, preferably dark colored bed sheets!' His voice boomed and echoed off the walls and into her ears. She was reminded of nails on a chalkboard, only deeper, and somehow meaner.

'Ok.' She pulled herself all the way back into the bedroom and went to the small linen closet in the bathroom. She pulled out the darkest set of sheets she could find. They were a reasonably dark blue, well; the tiny little flowers on them were anyway. They stood out nicely against the bright white background. They would have to do.

She returned to Latham with the sheets and handed them over. She turned and took a step toward the front door when he yelled.

'Stop! You aren't going anywhere. Plop your ass down in that chair and wait.'

She jumped as the echo of his voice boomed through the room. She turned and looked at him, finally coming to her senses enough to shake free of the fog she had been in. 'I think you can handle this. I don't know what happened, and I don't want to. I've stayed too long already. Thanks for helping me out of the shock, but I'll be going...'

Latham's hand came out of nowhere and met her face with a loud crack. 'I said sit!'

Her eyes burned as tears welled in them. The stinging in her right cheek caused her face to wince and her hand flew up to rub it. Stunned, she stood there, just staring at Latham. She couldn't believe he had struck her. She opened her mouth to curse him and tell him she would not be sitting.

The moment she opened her mouth, Latham turned and grabbed her, by both arms this time, and twisted her around on her feet to face the wall and shoved her straight toward it. He followed immediately behind her. She raised her hands to prevent herself from smacking the wall with her face.

Latham slammed up against her and smashed her hard against the wall. He leaned his face in close. Placing his mouth against her ear, he spoke. 'I told you to do something. From now on, you will do what I tell you, or pay the consequences. Do you understand?'

Sarah was pressed against the wall so firmly and he was applying so much pressure on her from behind that she could barely take in a breath. He held her there, the heft of his large frame crushing her, she couldn't speak. Her face was pressed against the wall so hard that she feared a simple nod would break her neck. She attempted to force a responsive uh-huh, but it came out as a garbled grunt.

Suddenly, the body on the sofa gasped for air and began to cough. Latham flew the few feet between him and the couch. He leaned over the man and began to whisper to him.

Sarah realized she was free but was frozen solid in the spot against the wall. When Latham didn't slam against her again, she turned around. She saw Latham leaning over the man on the couch, his hands on his arms, pressing them firmly into the cushion. The man's eyes were open and blinking and his chest rising and falling abnormally. Latham was whispering something to him.

Sarah covered her mouth and rushed over beside Latham. 'Shit, he's alive!' She shouted.

Chapter 4

They take their seats around the small table and tap mugs before a friendly game of chugging ensues. It was the ritual at the end of their weekly double date night at BullShots. There is one loud bang after another as they swallow and slam their mugs on the table. They scrunch their faces, celebrating their ability to choke down the warm, bitter brew. Sophie lets out a loud belch. Nate and Todd clap their empty mugs on the table

Sarah is sitting with her back to the front door. She is the last to slam her mug down, empty for a change. As the bitterness fades, she notices everyone is staring at the something behind her. Someone new has come through the door. Sarah turns around to see who is just now getting there fifteen minutes before they close. When she sees who it is, she gasps, turns back around and whispers, 'What is he doing here?'

Latham is standing in the doorway, eyeballing the crowd. It is obvious he is looking for someone. Sarah just knows it is her. Her heart begins to race and is pounding in her ears. He told her Saturday afternoon she was to make no contact with anyone until she heard from him again. She acknowledged it because he didn't leave her much choice at the time but that was when the guy on the couch was dead. He wasn't anymore.

She hadn't seen or heard a peep from him since she locked up the guest house behind him on Saturday. She assumed that he had taken the guy to the hospital, and the whole thing was over now. So why was he here? The questions went on and on.

Sophie tapped Sarah on the shoulder and Sarah about jumped out of her skin. 'Something you want to tell the rest of the class?

Sarah snapped back to the moment. She hadn't heard Sophie's question. It was like the world had stopped for a moment, but only for her. She looked around the table and saw and felt all eyes on her. She looked back toward Latham and then back to the table of friends in front of her. The panic peaked.

How am I supposed to handle this? There are three people in front of her who have no idea what's happened. It was over, so she didn't have any reason to be panicking. She was, though. She looked at Sophie, a pleading look on her face. Not sure what she was asking, but definitely asking something.

Sophie caught the look. 'Not someone you want to see I take it?'

Sarah shakes her head back and forth. The fear and panic are obvious on her face and a lump is stuck in her throat. She tries to clear it and says 'He's my dad's...associate. I don't know what he is doing here. I don't want to know. Ignore him?'

'Ok then. I'll just go tell him to go away.' Sophie stood up, tugged at the bottom edge of her blouse, and picked up her empty mug. 'Todd, darling, hold my beer.' She shoved the mug into her boyfriend's chest and she strode toward the door with a purpose.

Sarah's eyes grew wide. She opened her mouth to speak. 'No Sop..' Sophie was halfway across the large room before Sarah could protest. She had not intended for Sophie to go talk to him but she knew Sophie wouldn't take any shit. Sarah had seen her in action and knew better than to get between her and whatever she was going to go do. She watched in horror as Sophie strode up to the large man standing in the doorway still eyeing the crowd. She did not at all expect what happened next.

Sarah's stomach turned as she watched Sophie stroll up to Latham and strike up a conversation. She didn't know how good Latham's eyesight was and they were way in the back. She sank in her chair anyway. From the way he was still looking around, she was certain he had not seen her.

She watched, tension building inside her at the rate of tons per second. Sophie's gestures and Latham's reactions to them gave the impression that things were fine.

Until they weren't.

Latham, in a split second, shoved Sophie backward. An employee, standing nearby, took two steps and caught her by her arms before she hit the ground. Nate and Todd jumped to their feet, ready to bolt to her rescue. Sarah watched Sophie shoot them a negative glance and they spun their chairs around to face the door and calmly took their seats. Their eyes fixed on Sophie.

Sophie had never been one to take being manhandled lying down. She stood up, adjusted her blouse again, and stepped right back up to Latham. What she said before had set something off inside him, but what she said this time was the equivalent of dumping gasoline on an already blazing fire.

Latham, in a flash, balled up his fist and reared back to swing. The moment he released the full force of his punch, a hand caught his fist mid-air. A grabbed his arm and twisted it around behind him. He took a step forward and met Latham eye to eye. They exchanged words.

Latham relaxed and took a step backward. He shook his head and made a defensive gesture with his free hand and his lips moved. The bouncer released his hold but stayed between Latham and Sophie. More words were had and Latham side stepped the bouncer and lunged at Sophie again.

The bouncer locked Latham in a bear hug and lunged for the door, banging Latham against it. He held him there until Sophie moved forward and pushed the door open. The bouncer struggled with Latham but maneuvered him out the door. Sophie let it close behind them. She stood there, eyes wide, glaring through the glass door. Her head bobbed and then she nodded.

After a few moments, the bouncer came through the door and he and Sophie chatted like it was nothing. She gave him a quick hug before returning to the table.

Sarah, Todd, and Nate all sat with their eyeballs the size of saucers and their chins on the table. They had seen her take charge before, but continuing to challenge a total stranger. This was new even for her.

Chapter 5

Nate walks Sarah to her car. They chit chat about the nights events and Sarah hopes that he doesn't mention her reaction to the guy that Sophie ran off, but he does.

She tries to shrug him off. Nate pushes for an answer. She relents and tells him that the guy is a 'friend' of her dad's. She doesn't know that he was there for her, or why he would be. It just put her off that he was there at all. She is curious and kind of anxious to get home and see if her dad might know though.

Nate accepts that, but before he can ask any more questions, Sophie comes bouncing up to the car. She reminds them about the party at her house on Saturday.

She hugs Nate and tells him goodnight. Then she squeezes between him and the car door to get to Sarah. Sophie hugs Sarah. She tells her she loves her and whispers in her ear to call her tomorrow.

Sophie heads back inside while Todd says his goodbyes to Sarah and Nate. Sarah turns on her car and steps out of it to wrap her arms around Nate one more time. Her mind is a little scattered with questions about Latham and the events of the weekend.

She tries to push her thoughts aside and just be in the moment with Nate. She squeezes him tight and promises him a 'private date' next week. The hugging and kissing lingers. Neither of them want to let go. She hesitantly pulls away and slinks into the car. She blows Nate kisses as he closes the door and she backs away.

Sarah turns out of the parking lot and heads down the main road toward home. She reaches the first turn on her route not paying much attention to what is behind her.

High beams flashed in both the rear view and side mirrors. They almost blinded her completely. She flipped the little switch on the bottom of the review mirror and steered a little to the right to remove the glare from the side mirrors. She saw the silhouette of a large truck for just a second before the lights lined up with her mirrors again.

'Latham!' She yelled at no one as she steered a little to the left. The large vehicle lined itself up with her mirrors once more and the glare burned her eyes to the point of tears.

She didn't have to guess anymore. She knew for sure now that he had shown up tonight looking for her. A rage welled up inside her like she had never known. 'How dare he show up in my space and cause a scene like that, and then follow me. He is trying to intimidate me, and it isn't going to work.'

If she had any doubt about it being Latham, she wouldn't have stopped. Latham was a big guy, but her father was a powerful man and he could take care of this guy for her if it came to that, but she was a big girl now. She was going to fight her own battle. He was no stranger, and right here right now, she was going to give him what for. She did not get treated by people the way he treated her on Saturday, and he would not treat her like that again.

She steered her car to the grassy shoulder and made an immediate stop. He was driving close enough that she expected him to fly right on past her. Instead, he pulled and stopped a few feet behind her. His high beams glaring in both mirrors again.

Fire burned in her eyes and nostrils. She swung her door wide open and stepped out, slamming the door shut behind her. She stomped back toward the truck. She reached the driver side door at full steam.

The driver swung his door wide open at just the right moment. The door smacked her in the face, splitting her lip, and sent her flying backward. She landed flat on her back with a thud.

She rolled to her left side, trying to catch her breath. The landing felt like it forced every particle of oxygen from her body. She writhed around as the waves of pain ebbed and faded throughout her body.

A second later, Someone had her by her hair, pulling her to her feet. They shoved her forward and she collided with the front of the truck. She put her hands up just in time to keep her head from bouncing off of the headlight.

In a flash, she is slammed hard against the truck again. The plastic of the grill grating the skin on her bare arms. She felt the heat of the headlight through her shirt as her body slipped and slid across the truck. She didn't know what was happening until it happened.

She was pinned to the front of the truck. His arm was pressed into her back between her shoulders. She stood there helpless as he tugged and yanked at her pants and underwear. She had no leverage, or means to escape. She knew what was coming as she screamed 'Nooo!' Suddenly, fire spread through her nether regions.

Her chest ached as she was pressed against the grill again and again, and each thrust lifted her onto her toes. Her legs grew weak and threatened to buckle. The pace quickened and the force behind each thrust increased. Her screams sounded like whispers, drowned out by his grunting in her ear and the hum of the engine.

The whole thing lasted just a few moments. It seemed like an eternity for her. It ended with a final forceful thrust, holding her there, while he whispered in her ear. 'You stopped first. Willingly. You are a slut. One word about this and the world will know about your family's secret.'

The voice was unfamiliar. It was his truck, his asshole moves, but not his voice. And as far as she knew there was no secret. They guy lived. She was confused.

He pulled away from her and grabbed her by the back of her shirt. He turned her around and shoved her toward her own car, her pants still pulled down. She stumbled a few feet and caught herself with both hands on the trunk of her car. She stood there, her breathing erratic and her body on fire.

The wheels of the truck squealed against the soft grassy shoulder. Sarah stood there, disoriented and alone. Her black slacks and blue panties still down around her thighs. She started to cry. She pulled her clothes back into place and dusted herself off. She ran to the driver side of her car and jumped in, locking the doors around her. She buried her face in her hands and sobbed. When the hysteria cleared, she put the car into drive and cried all the way home.

Chapter 6

Sarah sat down on the floor next to the toilet for a long time. Disgusted by what had just happened, but more disappointed by her inability to defend herself. She unrolled some toilet paper and blew her nose.

She cleaned herself up, sat down on the edge of her bed and fought back tears. Tank was lying on her pillow, waiting. As soon as he heard her sniffle, he was in her lap, purring and nuzzling her. He was her best friend, and could dry up her tears like no one else. Solid black and about 35 pounds now, he was a large cat, and his long coat made him look even bigger.

He was as soft as silk and his purr would fill the entire space of her room. He only purred when he was in her lap, consoling her. It didn't happen very often but he would sit with two of his legs on each of her legs facing her. She would rest her head on top of his and he would purr while she stroked his back. Tonight, his purr was especially loud. She sat there petting him and letting the tears flow until she was in control again.

She tried to get back to what she had planned to do when she got home. Reflect on her night out with the gang. She closed her eyes and tried to picture Nate's face. His smiling face appeared in her mind and she smiled. She lay back on her bed and replayed the bits of the night that just he was in. Tank walked right across her chest to her pillow. He kneaded around in a circle a few times before settling, with a flop, on her pillow, still purring softly.

She recalled making that amazing 8-ball shot and not scratching the other night. A twitch of pride sizzled through her. She had a lot to be proud of. The bar was doing well. Nate was undoubtedly in love with her. Life was perfect. With the exception of Latham. She tried to fight the urge to think about him.

She forced a thought about Nate back into her mind. Her smile grew but then shrank again when her stomach flip-flopped. Latham's face cut in. His crude smile staring at her with those piercing blue eyes made her stomach churn.

Her eyes popped wide as the room swirled around her and a creeping feeling climbed up the back of her throat. She ran to the bathroom and heaved until her entire body cramped.

AS SHE SLID from a kneeling position to sitting beside the commode, she winced. She examined herself, sitting there on the floor. The pain in her midsection was near agony every time she took a breath. Bruises were already developing, deep and dark blue, on her midsection and on the underside of her forearms.

It was going to be difficult to hide the marks. The split in her lip wasn't too bad, the soreness of her tongue was already gone, but the rest would take a while to go away. She could explain the cut in her lip and the bruising on her forearms with a fall, she supposed.

She plugged up the drain in the tub and filled it with hot water. When it was about halfway full, she slowly sank down in it up to her ears. The hot water would help get rid of the dirty feeling, but mostly it just soothed her aches and help her relax and move on. She would just lay there and soak until she felt clean again.

Emptying the tub and refiling it two or three times, then shower. Tonight, it was going to be four, maybe five before she could relax. She didn't know if she would ever be able to move on.

Chapter 7

Sarah wakes up with Tank wrapped around her head snoring loudly for a cat. The doorbell was ringing. The chime box was right outside her bedroom door, so it was loud, and an unusual sound to wake up to. She bolts upright and looks back and forth around her room. She was dreaming about something, but she couldn't remember what. She hears the doorbell again.

She rolls out of bed and grabs her robe as the doorbell rings a third time. A long, slightly heavy, dark pink fleece, she wraps it around herself and winces as she yanks the tie tightly around her middle. She loosens it a bit and looks at her alarm clock. She tucks her feet into her slippers and heads for the door.

She works to recall what day it is. 'Eight o'clock on a Friday morning, seriously?'

The bell rings again. She picks up her pace down the stairs, yelling at the door. 'I'm coming, just hold on.'

When she gets to the door and looks through the window. She recognizes DJ, the package delivery guy, looking out into the yard. He is holding a long thin box in his arm like a scepter, an electronic clipboard in his other. She jerks the door open. She is usually a morning person, but this week has taken a lot out of her. Today, she is in no mood to deal with people. 'Morning DJ.'

He turns around and smiles a wide, attractive smile at her. He is a young man, a year or two older than her, broad at the shoulders, with strawberry blonde hair poking out the sides under his brown ball cap. His sky blue eyes were friendly and familiar. He filled out his brown uniform nicely in her opinion, but it was far from a good color for him.

'Good morning Sarah. Special delivery just for you.'

The tone in his voice reminded her of Mr. McFeeley from Mister Roger's Neighborhood. It was cheesy and delightful. It seemed rehearsed, and she wondered if he did on his entire route, or if it was just for her, but it always made her smile. Today was no different.

He leaned the clipboard toward her and rolled his eyes quickly. The view of her skin peeking through her robe would have been a pleasing thing to him most days. She had been answering the door to him for a few years. He had seen her in bikinis fresh out of the pool. Today though, the fact that it looked pretty deeply bruised concerned him. He looked her over as she signed for her packages. 'Are you alright Sarah? That bruising looks pretty bad.'

Sarah looked down at her chest. Her robe had slid open part way, exposing no vitally private parts, but the bruising across her chest was dark and obvious. She blushed. 'Oh Shit!' She grabbed the edges of her robe and pulled them tightly against her chest and tried to hide a wince. 'Yes, I'm fine. Fell up the stairs when I got home last night. Beat myself up pretty good. I'm such a klutz sometimes.'

'I apologize. I really wasn't trying to look or anything. The contrast of the colors caught my eye. I'm so sorry.' His voice was nervous and matched his apology. He had been delivering packages here regularly for nearly three years. She is a beautiful woman, and that may have been what caught his attention initially, but honestly, it was the black and blue under the dark pink that really pulled him in.

He didn't know a whole lot about the family, but he knew there was an older man here a while back that looked like he could be just enough of an asshole to do something like this to her. He had signed for a few packages for Mr. Rosenthal and was a real prick about it. He believed his name was Latham something. He didn't like him. He wouldn't pry, but he wouldn't have been able to live with himself if he hadn't said something. He chose his next words very carefully. 'I've been coming here for a few years now Sarah. I've not known you to ever be a klutz. Just know that if it is ever anything more than that, you are more than welcome to call me. I'll help you out in any way that I can.'

Sarah knew what he was implying, and she knew he was sincere. She panicked a little and hoped it didn't show. 'Oh no. It's nothing like that, thank you for being concerned, DJ. I drank a little too much last night with some friends, and when I got home, I tripped going up the stairs. Really, that's all that happened. My boyfriend, Nate is a really sweet and gentle guy, and mom and dad have not spanked me since I was like 8. I'm fine. Really'She handed him back the clipboard and held her hands out for the package in his arms.

He passed the tall box to her and smiled. 'I'm really sorry if I overstepped, Sarah. You are just way too pretty to be going around banged up like this. He tried to make sure that his face read just friendly concern, but his gut was telling him something completely different. 'The offer still stands. If you ever need it, I've got your back.' He winked at her.

She stood there, confused and flattered. She had never had anyone tell her these kinds of things. She didn't know how to respond. She smiled and stared at the ground. Thoughts sprang to her mind about how she didn't recognize the voice last night and she got really uncomfortable.

Her brain threw all kinds of stuff at her. Could this be the guy that did this to her? She thanked him for the delivery and stepped inside backward. Her eyes locked on him. He tipped his hat, turned and hopped off the porch and half skipped back to his truck.

She shook off the thought that it could have been this guy. She was certain that it was Latham and she wouldn't be convinced otherwise. The confusion was simply a result of shock from everything that was happening. It could only be him.

Chapter 8

She carried the box inside. Kicking the door closed with her toes, she headed for the kitchen. No one ever sent her packages. She did get one every so often for her birthday from her dad. Her birthday was months away still, though. Sparks of electricity rippled over her skin as she looked at the shipping label. It was from the florist shop in town.

She looked the tall box over, deciding how to open it. If it was flowers, she didn't want to lay it down. It was paper taped together all the way around, like a puzzle box. She grabbed a knife from the drawer in front of her and cut, very gently, all the way around. She got it open and what she found took her breath away.

It was flowers. A dozen of the most beautiful red roses she has ever seen or smelled. Their aroma filled her nostrils as soon as the box top lifted slightly. They had been wrapped in a sheet of deep red tissue paper and gold foil and placed inside a clear, etched, crystal vase. The whole thing was wrapped in a clear sheet of cellophane. Tears stung her eyes. 'Oh Nate.' A sigh slipped from his lips.

She pulled the vase out of the box gently, shoved the box to the floor, and set it gently on the counter. She turned it a full circle, just staring, in awe. No one had ever sent her flowers before, and the thought of them being from Nate had her breathless. She searched them for a card. She didn't find one. She was convinced they had to be from Nate.

They were deep mix of burgundies and reds and their fragrance filled her nose. He had done a great job picking them. She loved them. She would have loved them if they were a broken handful of daisies too, though. She contemplated the reasons that he would have sent them. He had been her teammate for a year and lost every game that she had, usually because of her. Or just a really sweet thing for him to do. It didn't matter, she was pleased.

She turned her attention to the box on the floor. There was a large envelope. Her name beautifully scripted in calligraphy on the front. She admired the art and commented on how beautiful it made her name look. It was a large card for what she expected. Not just one of those last minute, pulled off the shelf next to the florist counter, after thoughts. A real, heartfelt, stand there in front of the rack of hundreds until you found just the right one, card. A tear stung her eye.

She opened up the envelope and pulled out the card. The front was a beautiful rose. The card stock was heavy, high quality, with a plastic wrap over the front and back. 'Oh Nate!' She sighed. She opened it slowly and tenderly.

The first line made her want to vomit. 'Good morning slut!' Her visions of Nate painstakingly picking out each item dissolved. 'Latham. What the actual fuck?' Not just any flowers either, beautiful red roses and an expensive vase. She glared at them there on the counter. She strongly willed it all to burst into flames. She didn't bother reading the rest of the card.

She threw the card back in the box and started toward the back door, smashing the box to pieces. Olivia, her mother, waltzes into the kitchen. 'Oh my, what beautiful flowers. Where are they from?' Sarah stops in her tracks in front of the sink.

Sarah rolls her eyes. That's her mother, only concerned with where they are from, not who sent them. 'No one special,' she chokes on the words.

Olivia rubs a petal between her fingers and flicks the edge of the vase. It makes a high pitched ting against her manicured nail. She nods then turns toward the fridge. 'Pretty fancy and expensive stuff from...' She makes finger quotes in the air. 'No one special'.

She sets the jug on the counter and goes to the cabinet to Sarah's left to get a glass. She reaches into the cabinet to the right and takes out a large bottle of aspirin. She fiddles with the bottle for a moment, and then pushes it at Sarah. 'Open this.'

Sarah drops the box on the floor and kicks it toward the back door. She takes the bottle and opens it with ease. She pours two pills into her mother's hand.

Olivia looks at her and nods, 'two more.'

Sarah bounces two more pills out of the bottle into her hand, picks up the lid and screws it back on the bottle.

Olivia pops the pills into her mouth all at once and gulps down half her glass of orange juice. She starts to walk away but stops to call back over her shoulder. 'You should get those in some water before they wilt. Good taste that guy.' She leaves the room without another word.

Sarah wants to throw them on the floor and stomp all over them. After what he did to her, the last thing she wants is expensive gifts with offensive words attached.

She takes the vase of flowers to the sink, fills it with water, and sets it back in the center of the counter. She has no desire to have anything from Latham, but she isn't going to just kill flowers. She will just continue pretending they are from Nate. She picks up the empty box and carries it out to the trash.

She tosses the box in the recycle bin, passes a glance to the guest house and shivers.

She goes back upstairs and closes her door quietly. She flops down onto her bed. Tank comes from somewhere off the bed and head butts her. His purr was soft and quiet. 'How are you this morning, my handsome little devil?' She rubs his head and down his back a couple of times.

She rolls over on her back, staring up at the ceiling. All she could see was Latham winning every battle she fought with him. She wanted to cry.

Instead, she picked up the phone.

Chapter 9

Sarah heard four rings before Sophie's voice chimed in. 'Hey girly. What's up?' Sophie's voice was always comforting and cheerful. Sarah was impressed with her ability to carry one three conversations at once and never miss a lick in any of them. Sarah struggled to keep up with one conversation half the time.

They exchanged their regular chit chat and all was going well until Sophie mentioned her excitement about the weekend. Sarah had forgotten all about the party at Sophie and Todd's that weekend and started to panic. She had been looking forward to spending time with time with her friends. One night a week was never enough. The bruises would screw everything up though and she didn't know what she was going to do. She found herself making excuses for why she couldn't come.

'Ok, spill it!' Sophie blurted into the phone. 'What happened?' Sophie was great at catching on when something was wrong. Something was definitely amiss. 'I want to know everything.' She pressed.

Sarah didn't expect her to pick up on it quite so quick. She had no idea where to start or what to say. She sat, silent, for a few moments gathering her thoughts.

'Did you and Nate break up?' Sophie questioned, and then continued, answering her own question. 'No way. Todd would have known, and would have told me. Unless that is why you are calling...' Her voice trailed off.

'No, we didn't break up. I haven't talked to him yet today, but it's not that.' She was confident in the status of her relationship, at least until he saw the marks all over her. That might change things a bit.

'Well what the hell is it then?' Sophie pushed, impatient.

'I don't know, I think I might be getting my period.' She wasn't, but it was a good excuse for the hum drums if she ever had one.

'Bullshit! You were on your period last week. What it is? Don't make me come over there.'

Sarah knew she could really use her best friend right now. She wouldn't usually just come right out and ask Sophie to come over, but she sucked in a breath. 'Could you?'

'Could I what?'

'Come over here?'

'Oh... umm..., yeah. Are you ok?'

'Yeah, I'm fine. Just need to talk, and face to face might be...' Her voice trailed off. She didn't want to use the word 'easier'. She hoped that once Sophie saw the state she was in, Sophie would understand and take over.

She would only have to answer questions. She didn't know if she could explain the whole thing in detail without falling completely apart.

'Ok Sweetie. I'll be there shortly. See you soon.'

'Ok, thanks. See you.'

Sarah paced around her room. She knew she wouldn't have long to wait for Sophie to show up. She didn't know what she was going to say. Sophie would have all kinds of ideas, like putting Latham's balls in a vice or worse, once she found out what happened. She just wanted all of this to go away. She wanted her perfect life back.

She sat down on the edge of her bed. How much of the whole story she would or should tell Sophie plagued Sarah's mind. It wouldn't benefit anyone to have another person knowing about the incident. 'That isn't even an incident at all since the guy is alive'. She yelled at herself.

She couldn't hide the feeling of being violated. She didn't want to hide it. She was angry and knew that Sophie would vindicate her anger. She would probably be angry too. She needed to get this out and talk about it without being judged so she could pick herself up and move on. She knew Sophie was good for that. She got up and got dressed. Refusing to be depressed about it any longer.

When the doorbell rang, she put on her best smile and bounced down the stairs. She yanked the door open, ready to fly into her best friends arms for the warmest and most comforting hug. She stopped dead in her tracks, her rubber soled sneakers squealing on the freshly waxed hardwood floor. It wasn't Sophie standing there with open arms.

Sarah's face scrunched up and fire burned in her eyes. Latham was standing there. She flew at him arms flailing. She couldn't contain the rage that filled her. She pounded as hard as she could on him. His chest taking the blows like her hands were made of feathers. She punched repeatedly with every bit of strength that she had. She cursed and yelled at him. He just stood there.

She was so caught up in trying to turn Latham into ground beef that she didn't see Sophie arrive. She was completely oblivious of Sophie's presence until she had been pulled inside and Sophie was telling Latham that he should probably just leave. She was seeing things like they were a movie and she was watching from the dark.

Sophie didn't know who this guy was, but he had obviously pissed Sarah off. She looked back and forth between Sarah and Latham. Sarah stood there with her fists clenched and her nostrils flaring. This guy stood there with a smug but not confused look on his face. She stepped between them and looked him eye to eye. 'You should probably go. I'll see if I can get her calmed down.'

Sarah watched through tears. Latham nodded and turned to leave. Sophie closed the door behind him and turned to face her.

Fire burned inside of Sarah. She didn't know what had come over her. Her chest rose and fell and she could feel her heart racing in her chest and her head. Her fists were still clenched, and tears were streaming down her face. She wanted to die and she wanted to take him with her.

Sophie stepped away from the door and quietly placed her arms around Sarah. She had no idea why she had shown up and found Sarah beating on a man almost twice her size. She knew it had to be pretty bad, but she wouldn't get any answers until Sarah was calm. So she just stood there, hugging her, rubbing her back gently, until her head fell on her shoulder and she started to sob.

The sobs that flowed from Sarah were intense. She cried and cried and Sophie could feel her blouse being soaked through with tears. She didn't know what to do. She would stand here and hold her friend forever if that is what she needed, but she had a feeling that she needed so much more than that. She waited for the sobs to simmer before she spoke.

'I'm here now sweetie. It's ok. Let's go upstairs and talk.' Sophie coddled and urged her to look up.

Sarah nodded against Sophie's shoulder then pulled herself away. She turned toward the stairs. She sniffled and coughed. A dry, hacking, sound that ended in a loud dry heave echoed up ahead of her. She climbed the stairs and rounded the corner into her bedroom.

Chapter 10

Sophie plops down on the bed looking at Sarah. Sarah closes the door and turns to face Sophie. She takes a deep breath and carefully pulls the sleeves up over her arms. She lisft her shirt up to just above her bare breasts. The bruises across her chest and arms stand out blue and purple against her pale skin. She doesn't have the ability to actually speak. She stands there with her arms stretched out and her chest bare waiting for Sophie to speak.

Sophie's chin falls to the floor and her eyes expand to three times their normal size. Words come flying out of her mouth at a million miles an hour. 'What the hell? What happened? Are you alright? She jumps up and closes the gap between her and Sarah in a single stride. She takes one of Sarah's hands and pulls it away from her chest.

Sarah is still lost for words. Tears spill down her cheeks. The look on her face pleading with Sophie to just understand what happened so she doesn't have to say it out loud. She closes her eyes and tilts her head up toward the ceiling. Attempting to stifle a sob.

'Put the shirt back on. We can sit and talk. There is no need for you to be exposed like that.' She picks up the edge of Sarah's shirt and pulls it gently into place. They both sit down on the bed cross legged across from each other.

'Are you alright?' Sophie attempts to look Sarah in the eyes. Sarah looks away.

'Yes. No. I don't know.' Sarah choked the words out.

'Alright. Can you tell me what happened? How did you get the bruises?' Sophie coaxed.

'No.' It was a whisper.

'Ok. Can I ask questions and you tell me if I'm on the right track to figuring it out?'

Sarah nodded.

Sophie took Sarah's hand. 'Is this as bad as I think it is?'

Huge tears fell out of both of Sarah's eyes. She nodded twice and looked away. She ached from head to toe. Her chest heaved with every breath trying to contain the sobs that threatened to overtake her again.

Sophie squeezed Sarah's hand. 'I'm so sorry sweetie. Was it that guy?'

Sarah couldn't contain the ache anymore. She sobbed and howled. She still wasn't convinced that it was Latham. Something told her that it was, but things didn't match up. It looked like it could have been his truck, but she hadn't ever seen it that close up before. It could have been his voice but it seemed so unfamiliar to her, then the flowers being delivered this morning. None of it made any sense. She couldn't figure out why he would have done it in the first place. He knew her father and knew full well that he was a powerful man. Why would he even think to try? She sucked in several breaths. The pieces didn't fit together even when she threw in the guy her dad almost killed.

When her breathing settled. She said, 'I don't know.' Tears still falling in rivers from her eyes.

'You don't know? Then why were you pounding on him when I got here?'

'I thought he was you.'

'Lets try that again. Why were you pounding on him when I got here?'

Sarah took several deep breaths and a let out a long exhale. She wasn't making any sense and Sophie needed to know. She was going to have to talk about this. She held her breath for a moment and exhaled as hard as she could before speaking.

'Ok. I was ok when I thought it was you at the door. It wasn't and I got upset. I think he is the one that did this to me but it was dark and bright, I never saw his face, and I didn't recognize his voice, so...I don't know.'

'He talked to you during...'

'No. After. He reminded me that I was the one who stopped first when he was following me. Called me a whore.' The tears began to fall again.

'And you didn't recognize the voice at all?'

'No. I mean, it had to be him. He was the only one that had any reason to do that.'

'Who had any reas...Are you fucking serious right now?' Anger burned in Sophie's eyes. This was not the first time she had dealt with a rape victim. She had been right in this very spot herself once. She took a deep breath. 'I'm sorry. Let me rephrase that. No one ever gives someone else a reason to rape them.'

Sarah's eyes went wide and her stomach flopped. She jumped up and ran to the toilet. She heaved but nothing came up. She heaved again.

Sophie was at her side immediately and rubbed her back with one hand and pulled her hair back with the other. 'That was the first time you heard it said out loud isn't it?'

Sarah heaved again. She nodded her head before the next wave washed over her.

'Ok. Breathe. It will pass in a moment. You will be ok.' She spoke so softly and rubbed Sarah's back.

When Sarah was able, they went back and sat down on the bed.

Sophie took Sarah's hand again. 'Listen, we only have to talk about this as much as you are willing and able to. I'm here for you. I know it's awful. I also know that talking to someone will help. Just know that this isn't your fault and I still love you just as much as I did 10 minutes ago.'

Sarah rolled her eyes. 'Sometimes I forget that you were working on becoming a therapist before we bought the bar.' She squeezed Sophie's hand. 'I wish you would go back to it. You would be a great one.'

'Maybe I will one day. It's hard to deal with other people's problems on top of your own all the time. I like helping people, but it gets overwhelming. I just want you to be ok.'

'I'll be fine. I just need to get my life back under control. I don't want to let this get to me. I want to move on and just be fine.'

'I know you do. It doesn't work that way though. You gotta talk it out. Trust me.'

Sarah nodded. They talked for the next few hours until Sarah was able to laugh a little again. It did feel good to get things off of her chest. She still had deep concerns. The weekend at Sophie's house was probably the biggest one.

She needed to not think about all of it for a while. She also needed a drink or three.

'Can we get out of here for a while? I need to clear my head. Lets go to Crosstown's and dance or something.'

'It's two in the afternoon.' Sophie jabbed at her. 'Who starts drinking at 2pm? Who am I kidding, I would have already had a beer if I was at home. Let's grab some lunch on the way though. I'm starving.'

'Sounds like a plan.'

They took turns showering and got ready then headed out for a girls night on the town.

Chapter 11

Sarah and Sophie get back to Sarah's house later that night. They are giggling and hanging on to each other all the way into the house.

Latham and Jacob are standing in the entry way when the girls come in the front door. Jacob greets them with, 'Did you girls have a good time?'

They chuckle and nod. 'Yeah. We had fun. I really needed that.' Sarah glares at Latham as she says it and then drops her head and laughs with Sophie some more. 'I should probably go lay down though. My head is starting to spin.'

Jacob eyes Sophie. 'Had a little to drink then?'

Sophie catches his meaning. 'Yes, sir. We did. I less than her.'

'So who drove you home?' Jacob questioned.

'Ummm, I did sir.' Sophie confessed.

'But you had been drinking. Why didn't you call me? I would have sent Latham to get you. Neither of you needs a DUI. I won't pull any strings for you. Next time, call me.'

Sarah scoffed. 'We made it just fine, dad. No worries. I don't need you bailing me out. I really need to go lay down. Soph, help me up the stairs?'

'I trust you will be staying the night to sleep it off then Sophie or were you planing to go ahead and drive home too?'

Sophie was caught off guard. She hadn't intended to spend the night with Sarah. Todd was waiting for her at home. She knew Mr. Rosenthal wouldn't allow it as long as she had been drinking, though. 'I hadn't intended on staying sir, but I guess I can.'

'You guess you can? Have you been drinking or not?'

'Umm, not much. I had a White Russian and a few beers earlier. I'm alright though. I drove here just fine.'

'I see. So you just told me that you drove while drinking, and are planning to do it again?'

'Oh, well...umm...no sir.' Sophie back peddled. 'I, um,' she looked at Sarah and then at Latham. 'I don't want to impose sir and Tank's fur makes it hard for me to breathe while I sleep, so I just planned to go on home.'

Sarah piped up. 'Tank has never been in the guest house. You can crash there after you haul my ass up those stairs so I can lay down. Will that work dad?'

'That will do. Good night ladies. I'm just seeing Latham out.'

Latham's just stood there grinning the whole time and never said a word. Sophie knows that Latham is scheming. She can see it on his face. She knows he is still probably livid with her for kicking him out of the bar the other night but she is more concerned with him doing anything else to Sarah. 'Well, good night to you both then. I'll see myself to the guest house after I get her settled in.'

She helped Sarah up the stairs and into her room. When she came back down stairs, the lights were out and no one was about. She kicked off her heels and headed out the back door to the guest house.

SOPHIE TURNED THE FAUCET OFF, bent forward and ran her hands back and forth through her hair, then ran her hands like a squeegee over her entire body. She opened the door and grabbed a towel. She wrapped it around her head. She reached out and tugged the other one into the stall with her. She dried herself off and stepped out on to the rug. She paused for a brief moment, and looked around.

She thought she heard something and braced herself against the shower door for a moment. She felt like someone was there with her, but she ignored it. She was prepared for this. She stepped over in front of the sink and took the towel off of her head. She pulled a small pick out of her purse on the counter and poked and pulled it through her damp hair.

She wiped the mirror down. That's when she saw him. Sitting on the edge of the bed, picking up and smelling the clothes she had neatly folded and placed there. She froze for a split second. He dropped her panties, nonchalantly, when he noticed that she had spotted him.

Neither of them said anything for a long moment. Sophie spoke first. She had only half expected him to show up but she was prepared. 'So, what brings you to the guest house so late. Did you get scolded by Mr. Rosenthal for drinking and driving too?' She didn't look at him.

'Jacob asked me to unlock the guest house since I have his key. I never actually left. Just pulled my truck around back. Were you expecting me?'

His question made her nervous. If he had been here watching her the whole time, he would have seen her place the knife under the towel on the counter before she showered. Panic washed over her.

She answered his question with sarcasm. 'Absolutely. I always hope that a total stranger will be sitting on the bed waiting for me after a shower at my best friends guest house.'

Her expression never faltered. She turned her back to the sink and looked directly at him. She stared hard at him, challenging him almost. As long as she could stay in control of the situation, she would come out of this unscathed. She could not say the same for him.

He met her stare. 'I had to go get some supplies or I would have been here sooner.' He reached behind his back and held up a package of zip ties. He waved them at her.

She stifled a laugh that came out as a snort. His attempt at frightening her was over the top obvious and her panic subsided to hear he had not been here the whole time. She ran with it. 'Ohhhh, nice. You brought toys. Am I supposed to just put my hands together and let you tie me up?' She taunted him. 'I'm afraid you will be disappointed if you think I'm that easy to get.

He smirked; she was challenging him. This time she wouldn't have a bouncer to save her. He didn't like her from the moment he met her at the bar the other night. She was crass and rude and he was looking forward to putting her in her place this time.

She could see flames blazing in his eyes. That was exactly what she wanted to see. Why he was there was plainly clear and she would be ready for him. Since he had not made a move yet, she turned it up a notch. 'Or were you going to tie yourself up for me? I'll bet you are dying to find out what I could teach you.'

His eyes went dark and his nostrils flared. He would not be gotten the better of by this bitch again. With quickness he flew from the bed to her in a single stride. His hands were around her throat in an instant. The force he hit her with made her choke slightly. She was ready for him though. While he was taking that step toward her, she put her hands behind her back and picked up the buck knife she had sitting under the towel, just in case.

She brought it up and sank it deep into his left arm. She twisted it back and forth slightly and pulled it back out. She brought her hands up and waited for his next move.

His eyes went wide and his hands lost their grip on her neck. His right hand flew up to his shoulder as he yelled. 'Owwww!'

His arm stung. He had no idea what had happened until he felt his shirt getting wet and sticky under his hand. Then he saw her hands, and the knife that she held onto dripping with blood.

She gave him a bring it on look and beckoned him with her empty hand. She was ready for him.

He was in shock for a moment and his left arm was going numb, but his anger quickly took over again. He brought his blood soaked hand up and toward her face. Her empty hand blocked the move.

He growled and grabbed her by the arm and spun her around. Before she knew what happened, he had her looking at herself in the mirror and her lower body pinned against the counter.

He had hoped she would land on her own blade as he turned her and shoved against her. Tt might have been a successful maneuver if had managed to bend her over at the same time. She was more prepared than he expected and stood upright.

Her lower half was pressed against the counter, but her hands were not pinned underneath her as he had hoped. They were on the counter in front of her. The bloody knife still in her right hand. She was pinned but still not completely immobilized and that knife was a problem. He had to move quickly.

In a single move, he stepped into her with his good arm across her back, bending her over so her face was down on the counter. He kicked his knee up between her thighs, lifting her off the floor and heard her grunt. Her feet settled on the rug with her legs spread. He unfastened his pants and slid them down far enough to expose himself and pressed against her. He grabbed the arm with the knife and held it firmly.

The towel had slid up just so and was barely hanging over her bare ass. She felt his skin against hers. She clenched as hard as she could and waited for him to attempt to plunge deep into her forcefully. After a solid moment of nothing happening she noted, since he was pressed firmly against her, things were not at all firm. She couldn't contain the guffaw. 'Ha!'

He growled shoved himself against her hard. Her knees banged against the doors below the sink and she winced but laughter was boiling just below the surface. He grunted and slid his free hand between his hips and her bare ass. He fumbled with and shook his limp dick against the skin between her thighs.

Sophie is trying so hard not to laugh. She should have been raped and tossed aside already. She has now been standing here against the sink, face pressed hard on the counter, arms at her sides, for several minutes. She couldn't help herself. She taunted him. 'Why don't you go get the zip ties love, I'll wait right here.' She laughed out loud. Partly at the humor of her statement, but partly because of how her words sounded with her face stuck to the counter.

Ire burned inside him. He would have this woman if it killed him. 'What the fuck?!' he growled. 'You're supposed to be hard as a board for this. Cooperate dammit!'

She lost it. She was unable to contain the laughter any longer. Her body writhing in front of him. She didn't care that he was mere inches from having her. She was totally in control of the situation. 'Let me up Latham and I'll let you walk on out of here. It's over. Hang it up and go home.'

He stood there, shaking his lifeless cock vigorously. Frowning now. He couldn't even be angry anymore. He let go of the towel he was holding around her and backed away slowly.

She spun around to face him. Not taking a chance at him finally finding his libido and finishing what he started. She kept her blade between them. She didn't need to add any more insult to this fiasco. She looked at his arm. He was bleeding pretty badly. Her back, the counter, the floor, everything was blood soaked. 'We need to stop that bleeding or you are going to pass out. She bent down and picked up the towel that had fallen to the floor under her, balled it up and started toward him.

He shoved her away from him, pulled up his pants, and left without another word. Blood dripped from his hand and left a trail through the house as he went.

Sophie collapsed on the floor laughing hysterically. She was shaking. The outcome was hilarious, but she was completely shaken by how close she had actually come to being raped. This guy was bad news from the word go. She had no doubt now that it was him that raped Sarah even if she was unsure.

Suddenly, she covered her mouth with her hand and lunged for the toilet. She wretched for what seemed like hours. When she was finally able to stop, she looked around. There was blood everywhere. The vanity had blood smeared all over it and there was an obvious puddle on the floor right in front of it. Now, there were hand and footprints that tracked it all the way to the toilet and each side of the commode had bloody hand prints.

She reached up and pulled the handle. She didn't want to see that for fear that it would make her start hurling again. Cleaning this up was going to take forever.

At last, she stepped into the shower and turned the faucet on. She stepped under the waterfall before she even adjusted the temperature. As it heated up, she adjusted it blindly. She sat down on the floor of the shower and let the hot water wash away the blood, and the awful thoughts that plagued her now.

Then the thought hit her. What if Latham came back, with police? 'He's not that stupid.' She told herself. She needed to get out of here.

She frantically dug her keys out of her purse in the driveway and got into her car. She took a very deep breath, looked behind her, put the car in reverse, and backed out of the driveway. She realized right about then that she totally wasn't the slightest bit tipsy anymore. She drove home without incident.

Chapter 12

Latham left the guest house the way he had come but now he was bleeding.

The world was starting to spin. He needed to stop the bleeding, and soon. He was almost wishing he would have at least accepted the towel that the scheming bitch had offered him.

He had already taken enough of her ridicule for one day, and then some though. He looked around the back for a t-shirt he knew was there somewhere. He immediately pressed it to his shoulder. This was going to need stitches and maybe a sling. He would have to drive himself to the emergency room.

He laid his head back on the seat. He turned sideways in his seat and pressed his arm against the seat, holding the t-shirt against his wound. He opened the center console and dug around until he found a roll of duct tape.

He fumbled with the end for just a moment. He wrapped it around the shirt and his arm several times and then up over his shoulder for good measure. He bit into the tape and ripped it clean across.

He drove in the direction of the hospital. He had to concentrate really hard to keep his truck in one lane. He was trying to work out in his head how long he had been bleeding. 'Fuck!' He yelled. The hospital was another 7 minutes away. He started to panic.

He drew in a deep breath and floored it. He slid into a parking spot, threw the truck in park ran like a zombie, his good arm across his chest holding firm pressure on the wound, and his bad arm dangling at his side.

He burst through the emergency room door and straight to the desk. The woman at the window slid a clipboard over and told him he needed to sign in and take a seat.

He cursed and then took a deep breath. 'Look lady, I'm about to bleed to death. I was stabbed about 30 minutes ago and I'm about to pass out.' His chest heaving with every breath, sweat pouring down his face, he placed his good hand up to his neck to check his pulse.

The woman at the desk finally looked up at him. 'Sir, you will definitely pass out if you don't relax and take a seat." She looked back at her computer screen and typed away.

She had looked directly at him and had no concern for his predicament at all. He started to argue with her. 'I'm not going to sit down and wait. Get someone out here to see me now!' She took her glasses of, rubbed the bridge of her nose between her thumb and forefinger for a moment. She mumbled 'Lord help me not kill this man.' She looked right at him with a smile on her face and glared at him. She took a deep breath before she spoke as kindly as she could.

'Sir, I recognize and acknowledge that you are bleeding. Since you are standing here in front of me, making me aware that you have been bleeding for 30 minutes, I am going to assume that a major artery was not hit, in which case you would have bled out twenty-five minutes ago, I think it is safe to assume that you will be alright a few more minutes. Please sign in right there and take a seat!' She put her glasses and went back to typing.

Latham started to speak again. She turned her head toward him slowly and peered at him over her glasses. Her eyes moved from his to the sign in sheet. He opened his mouth to speak but thought better of it.

He scribbled his name on the form and found a seat. He leaned his head back and waited for his name to be called.

Within about fifteen minutes, he was triaged and put in a room to see a doctor. He waited another 5 minutes and there was a knock on the door. The doctor, an older man, in blue scrubs and a white pocketed lab coat stepped in and introduced himself. 'Hi there. I'm Dr. Franklin. How are you feeling?'

He was followed by a police officer. Latham was confused. 'Why were the cops here? Had that little bitch called them? She would pay for all of this.'

Panic slid up Latham's throat as he asked, 'why is he here?'

'Well, when you report to the nurse out front that you have been stabbed, we bring in law enforcement and they take a statement.'

Latham breathed a sigh of relief. The bitch hadn't called the cops on him. He still hated her.

'Oh, well, I was stabbed.' He had to think quickly. 'Well, I have a stab wound. It's not anything I need to press charges over or anything. I stabbed myself. It was a careless accident.'

The officer and the doctor both looked at him suspiciously. The doctor asked. 'If it was an accident, why did you come in saying someone stabbed you?'

Latham stared at the floor. In his head he was running through scenarios that would make sense as to how he "accidentally" stabbed himself in the shoulder. He almost didn't hear the question.

'What? Oh, I thought I was dying and that it would get me in here quicker.' It was the truth. He was bleeding and feeling light headed. He had been stabbed and had lost a lot of blood.

'Well, let me take a look.' The doctor had been gathering up supplies out of various drawers and cabinets around them. He cut through the tape and peeled the shirt away from his arm. He then pinched the sleeve of his expensive dark blue shirt and was about to cut into it.

'Is that necessary?' Latham asked. He could have just stood up and took the shirt off.

'Only if you want me to look at the wound. Would you like to unbutton the cuff and roll all the way up here?' He pointed to the top of his shoulder.

The idea of rolling his sleeve all the way up over the wound made him cringe. 'No, I suppose I don't. Go ahead. It's just, it's an expensive shirt.'

The officer started asking questions. 'Hot date that didn't go according to plan?'

Latham smirked. 'I guess you could say that.'

'Is that how this happened? You had a fight and she stabbed you?' The officer continued questioning.

'No, no. Not at all. I had already dropped her off when this happened. I was doing some work on the electrical system in my truck.' he lied. I noticed a short on the way to pick her up. I pulled out my knife to work on it and laid it on the seat. When I leaned over, to reach for the wires under the passenger side, I leaned on the blade.'

'Mmmhmmm' the doctor was putting a Band-Aid over the wound. 'Three stitches and you're all fixed up.'

'Three stitches??? That's it?'

'That's it.'

'It bled a lot. I thought I was dying. My arm went dead. How did it only need 3 stitches?'

'Well, it's in the muscle, rich with blood, but you missed any major arteries. I don't know why your arm went dead. I'm not seeing any nerve damage. See if you can move your fingers.'

Latham wiggled all of his fingers.

'Good, now bend your arm.'

He bent his arm, and winced, but the arm moved.

'Ok, good. The pain is because you are moving the muscle that has been injured. It will be sore for a few days, but you should be fine. Rate the pain on a scale of 1-10 for me, 1 being no pain, 10 is the worst pain you have ever felt.'

'About a 4 I suppose, unless I move it. Then it's about a 5.'

'Ok, you can take some ibuprofen for the pain if it is too bothersome, but that's about all I can do for you.' He ripped his gloves off, tucked one into the other, and tossed them in the trash can in the corner.

'Alright, thanks doc.' He shook the doctor's hand and the doctor left the room.

The officer looked him over. 'So what made you wait so long to come in?'

'I couldn't get the bleeding to stop. Look. I know I made a big deal about this when I came in. I really was scared that I was going to die. There was a whole lot of blood. That's all.'

'Alright. Well, next time be more careful where you lay your knife. Oh, and try not to aggravate the bear at the front desk. You have a good night.'

'You too officer.'

The officer left the room. Latham looked at his arm. Did he seriously think he was going to die from a wound that took all of 3 stitches? He couldn't move his arm, and his dick wouldn't work. Surely there was some kind of permanent damage.

He picked up his paper work and slowly walked back to his truck. At his truck he opened the door and stared at the blood that was smeared all over the place. He looked around in the back of his truck for another shirt or something he would wipe the blood up with. He didn't find anything. 'Shit.' He cussed out loud and climbed into his truck and started it up.

Latham drove home and parked in his driveway. He got out of the truck and headed for the door. He had the keys in his stabbed arm and used it just fine to unlock and open the door. He cussed again.

He told himself that he was not that big of a pussy. He never reacted to pain that way. He couldn't justify why he acted the way he did. He was angry. So angry. His adrenaline should have been boiling, and not felt any pain at all. He would have to explore this later, but right now, he needed a shower. He would get his truck detailed in the morning.

He dropped his keys in his pocket and closed the front door. He took three steps to his left and reached for the switch on the lamp. The room lit up. He looked around. Everything seemed to be in place.

He turned and walked to his kitchen and opened the fridge. It was fully stocked, with beer, supplement shakes, and Styrofoam boxes. He pulled out a beer and popped the top. He lifted the top on one of the Styrofoam boxes and quickly dropped it. Whatever was in it was unrecognizable now. He closed the door and walked back to his bedroom.

His home was a small place. It was a two bedroom in a small triplex. Clothes were strewn everywhere. He had a good habit of just leaving his clothes wherever he took them off. He had to slide an empty beer can over to make room for the one in his hand. There was a collection of them scattered around the room.

He was a slob. No doubt about it. 'I'll clean it up tomorrow.' he said to himself. He stripped out of his shirt and tossed it in the trash can next to the dresser. He picked up the beer and headed into the bathroom. He leaned over and turned on the hot water for the shower, to let it warm up, and then walked into the bedroom across the hall.

He stood at the foot of the bed and eyed the man lying there and took a sip of his beer. The guy had not moved. The blankets were still neatly tucked under him, exactly the way he had left him the night before. His eyes were closed and he looked so still. Latham walked over and checked man's neck for a pulse. He found one. Latham shrugged, took another drink, and turned to leave. 'I'll feed you in the morning if you are still alive' he said and pulled the door closed behind him.

Chapter 13

Sarah wakes up around 9am and heads to the guest house. Sophie is already gone. Sarah, being the one that cleans the guest house on a regular basis, notices the strong smell of bleach, and looks around.

The bed hasn't been slept in, and every towel in the place is in the bathroom sink. Bloody.

Sarah runs back to the house, grabs her phone. No missed calls, from Sophie or anyone else. She dials Sophie's number and waits for her to answer.

Todd answers. Sarah's heart starts racing. She blurted out her question. 'Todd, where is Sophie?"

'Good morning to you too Sarah. She's in bed, asleep. She got home really early this morning. Why?'

Sarah took a deep, relieved breath. 'I'm sorry. Good morning Todd. It was late when we got home, so she stayed over in the guest house. Is she alright?"

'As far as I can tell, she is. She came in about 5:30 this morning. Looking very tired, and just fell into bed. Something I should know about?'

'No, I guess not. Just have her call me when she gets up please?'

'Sure will. You still coming tonight?'

She had forgotten all about spending the weekend at Sophie's. She got excited. She wasn't going to miss it. Especially if Nate was going to be there. "With bells on. Nate's coming too, right?'

'Well, I haven't talked to him yet today, but the last time we did talk, he said he would be here after work tonight. It shouldn't be too late, around 7pm or so.'

'Great! So what is one the agenda for the weekend?'

'Board games and beer mostly. We have Cranium, Yahtzee, a deck of cards, Phase 10, and this new game that she got, but I don't remember what it's called. There's no telling what else we could get into.'

'This is true. Sophie always has something going on in that head of hers. It should be a lot of fun. What time should I show up?'

'Well, I'm going to let her sleep another couple of hours if she stays asleep that long. We have some prep to do, so I guess around 4 or so would be good. I'll have her call ya when she gets up though and give you a better idea.'

'Alright, thanks. I'll see you guys this afternoon then.'

'Ok. See you soon. Bye.'

'Bye.'

She breathed a sigh of relief again. Sophie was alive. That was all she really needed to know. She was still curious as to what happened.

She went back to the guest house and wrung out and gathered up the towels. She took a much closer look around. She didn't find anything but the bloody towels in the bathroom. She assumed they had to be blood. Just to be sure, she pulled the comforter back on the bed and checked the sheets. They were just as clean as they were when she changed them 2 days ago.

She replaced the comforter and readjusted the pillows, and picked up the towels and carried them to the main house. She would have to have them clean and back in the cabinet before she left for the weekend.

Olivia was in the kitchen when she came in through the back door. She noticed the pile of what were once white towels in Sarah's arms. 'What happened there?'

'I'm not exactly sure. Sophie stayed in the guest house last night and this morning, she was gone but I found these. She's at home sleeping now. Todd says she is fine. So, I don't know.'

Normally, Olivia would make a snide comment. She let it slide. Sarah looked her mom over. She almost didn't recognize her. At the moment, she appeared to be sober. She looked unusually old and run down this morning, but she was definitely sober. Sarah didn't spend much time with Olivia, but what little she did, she knew she didn't look like this.

'Are you alright mom? You look a little off this morning.'

'Yeah, I'm fine. Long night at work.' She yawned.

Sarah wasn't used to seeing her mom like this. Their exchanges were usually a bitter banter about how Sarah should be doing more to better herself or how disappointed she was that her only daughter opted to quit school and open a pool hall. She didn't know how to respond to this.

'Well, I better get these in the wash. I've got a lot to do before this afternoon.'

'What's going on this afternoon?'

'I'm going to Sophie's for the weekend. Just a cozy little get-together, me, Nate, her, and Todd.'

'Who's Todd?'

'Sophie's boyfriend.'

'Oh.' She nodded. She picked up her tall, half-full glass of orange juice and headed toward the stairs. 'Well have fun.'

'Alright.'

Sarah darted into the laundry room and started the towels to wash. She turned the signal on the washer so it would let her know when they were done. Then she headed up the stairs to shower and get dressed for the day.

After her shower, she went down to change the towels over to the dryer. There was a few minutes left on the cycle so she went into the kitchen to make herself some breakfast.

She popped two slices of toast into the toaster, and pulled the peanut butter out of the cabinet and set it on the counter. She went to the fridge and pulled out the strawberry jam, and set it on the counter. She pulled a butter knife out of the drawer and a paper plate out of the cabinet above her. She set the plate down and waited about 45 seconds and the toaster popped.

She slathered peanut butter and jelly on both slices of toast. She picked up the first one and took a bite and the buzzer on the washer went off. She skipped into the laundry room and switched the clothes over. She returned to her breakfast and was sad that her toast was now cold. She nibbled her way through the rest of the first slice. The peanut butter was now thick and dry. She went to the fridge and pulled out the carton of milk. She poured herself a glass and set the carton down in front of her. She checked the time on the microwave. It was barely 10am.

She was anxious about her upcoming visit but excited. She hadn't spent the night with Nate in a while. She was nervous and excited all at the same time. She couldn't wait.

She checked on the towels. Still 20 minutes to go. She cleared her breakfast away and headed upstairs to kill some time figuring out what she was going to take with her for the weekend.

She bolted up the stairs and into her room. When she got there, her phone was ringing. She picked it up and pressed the talk button, but was too late to catch the call. She called Sophie right back.

'Hey Soph! I was downstairs doing laundry. Are you alright, how did your night in the guest house go?'

'Yeah, I'm fine. It was pretty uneventful, why?'

'Well, let's start with the bloody towels?'

'Oh that.' There was an unusually long pause. 'Yeah, I'm fine.' Another long pause.

'I stubbed my toe and ripped off the nail. It bled all over the place before I even knew I was bleeding. I'm really sorry.'

'It's alright. It all seemed to come out. No harm done. Just glad you are ok, and it wasn't anything worse.'

'Pffft. I told you not to worry about me. So, you're still coming to the party for the weekend, right?'

'Yep. What time should I be there and more importantly, what should I bring?'

'Well, we have the food and beverages taken care of already. Nate won't be here until around 7, so unless you want to stand around and watch us 'cook' there really isn't any point in showing up earlier than five.' Sarah could picture Sophie winking at her. Sarah rolled her eyes.

'Five...really?'

'Yeah, what's wrong with five?'

'Nothing. I'm just already having a hard time figuring out what to do with myself until then.' She chuckled.

'Oh, well, you know you can come over anytime, but things won't be ready and the excitement won't start for a few hours yet.'

'I can probably hold off until around three or four. What should I pack?'

'Pack??? Are you running away from home? It's for one overnight. Just bring what you absolutely cannot do without for a night. Oh, on second thought, you might want to bring something a bit sexy, just in case.' Sophie snickered and then laughed out loud. 'Nate will be here.'

'Not funny. I don't want to kill the poor boy.' Sarcasm rolled off her tongue.

Sophie choked, then spit, then choked some more. 'Holy shit woman! That was fantastic. Where did that come from? You made me choke on my Dr Pepper.'

'I don't know. It was good wasn't it.' Sarah laughed.

'Well, be careful with it. It's a double-edged sword sometimes. You just damn near killed me with it.' 'I'll see you between three and four then. Have fun until then.'

'You too. I'll see you soon.'

Sarah hung up the phone and set it on the nightstand. She sat down on her bed and pulled a notepad and pen out of her nightstand. What could she not live without for one night? She made a list.

*toothbrush*cell phone*clean underwear*change of clothes*Tank

She figured she could go one night without Tank sleeping on her head. She scratched Tank off the list. She scribbled in "silky things" She pictured Nate's face as she pranced around in front of him dressed in silk panties and a matching top. She smiled.

She went to her closet and searched through the back looking for a bag to put everything in. She found a small backpack and set it out on her bed. She grabbed the silky things out of her dresser and stuffed them in the bottom of the bag before she lost her nerve. Then she remembered the towels. She darted out the door and down the stairs to the laundry room.

The dryer had stopped. She folded them up and carried them back out to the guest house. She looked around the house again. Something about Sophie's 'uneventful' and bloody towels didn't add up.

She didn't find anything out of place. . She went back to the towels and put them in the cabinet. She took one more look around. Sophie had done a great job of cleaning up. The only evidence of anything that had been left behind was now clean and back in the cabinet.

She shrugged. She pulled the door closed behind her and headed back to the main house. She noticed some red splotches on the ground in the grass in front of her before she took her first step. She looked around. She found more splotches to her left. She followed them all the way to the gate. She knew at that point since Latham and her dad were the only ones that have a key to that gate that it had to be Latham's blood. She would have to make Sophie tell her what really happened later on.

She was a little upset that her best friend would lie to her. She understood it to a point, but when she asked her outright, she lied. She would get to the bottom of it. If Latham hurt her, she needed to know about it. Doing it to her was one thing. Doing it to someone else was inexcusable.

She stomped back to the main house.

Chapter 14

When Sarah got back to her room, she picked up her phone and pulled up Sophie's phone number. She was about to hit the call button when an interesting thought crossed her mind. *Was it Latham that was bleeding?* Maybe she taught him a lesson? Wouldn't have been the first one she had taught him last night. Maybe it wasn't so much a lie as downplaying the truth. She was curious as to what actually happened, and she would ask, but until then, she would just assume that Sophie handled it and handled it well.

Her excitement returned, doubled. Now she was excited about getting away for the weekend, and even more excited to find out how Sophie had handled Latham alone. Sophie was constantly saying she was a big girl and could handle herself. Now, she believed it. Sophie was her new hero.

This evidence breathed a new sense of life into Sarah. If Sophie could take charge and teach Latham a lesson, why couldn't she? She has become afraid. Sophie wasn't scared at all. Why?

At that moment, Sarah decided that the last thing she was going to do was let Latham ruin her weekend. She just wanted her life to get back to normal, forget about her father's hands on that man's neck, Latham assaulting her, and just get on with her life.

Her spirits lifted and gave her a new energy. She needed to do something with it. She thought for a moment, and then she picked up her phone and opened her music player. She tapped her favorite playlist and hit shuffle all. The music started and she set the phone back down on the nightstand.

She went into the bathroom and gathered up her toothbrush, and some makeup. She walked back to the backpack she had pulled out of the closet. She set the items down and opened the backpack. She stuffed the items in on top of the lingerie and moved to her dresser.

Opening the bottom drawer, she shuffled through the jeans she had there. She pulled out a pair that she thought she might want to wear and tossed them to the bed. She went a drawer up and searched through it for the shirt she wanted to wear. She tossed it to the bed as well.

She then opened her top drawer on the right and stood there for a moment. She had several matching bra and panty sets to choose from. She usually didn't care if they matched. Tonight, though, depending on how things went, she wanted to make certain that she was well put together. She pulled out a black and a blue set. She tossed them both toward the bed.

She hadn't really noticed it, but she was sauntering and dancing around the room. She usually stayed as quiet as possible in her room. Habits die hard from her childhood. Playing music too loudly would most often bring howls from Olivia to turn it down, no matter how low it was playing. Today, she didn't care. She was going to play her music, and dance, and sing.

Sarah danced over to her bed and picked up the clothes off the floor and set them on the bed. Kid Rock's F.O.A.D is playing on her phone. She is singing along as she separates what she is going to wear today from what she is going to pack for the weekend.

She goes back to the closet to see what else she wants to take with her. She browses through the clothes hanging there, hesitates on a couple of different tops for a moment and moves on to the pants. Nothing there really either. Her gaze moves to the floor. She reaches down and pulls out a pair of black boots. Not her most expensive pair of shoes, but she loves them. They are soft and warm, with a flat heel, and a drawstring at the top. She carries them over to the bed.

She starts picking up and folding the clothes she is going to pack. She moves the undies to the side, still uncertain if they are what she wants to take with her. She picks up a pair of jeans, rolls them up and stuffs them in the bottom of the backpack. She does the same with the t-shirt. She looks at the boots she just took out of the closet and looks at the t-shirt in the backpack. She pulls it out and holds it up in front of her, deciding if the boots really go with this particular shirt.

She decides that it will do and rolls it up and stuffs it back in the backpack. She is singing and bobbing her head to the music while holding up and examining the blue bra and panties when she hears a voice at her bedroom door that nearly gives her a heart attack.

'Where do you think you are going?' Latham's voice boomed from her doorway.

If she had been a cat, her claws would have been sunk deep into the ceiling. She would be hanging there, upside down, trembling with fear. She is not a cat, so she stood there, frozen for a moment. Her horror, at the moment, was from being caught singing out loud and holding her underwear up in the air. Then the realization that Latham was standing there scared the shit out of her.

He never came upstairs. Ever. Why was he standing at her bedroom door now? 'What are you doing here?' She quickly tucked the bra and panties into a side pocket of the backpack. Attempting to hide her shock, she tried to move on like this was normal for her and that he wasn't standing there watching her.

She tried to ignore the embarrassment of the state of her bedroom, not necessarily from Latham being there, but from a man being there at all. She wasn't a slob, but there were clothes out of place and she felt a bit self-conscious. She ignored the question and browsed around, knowing something was missing from her packing list. 'Socks, I need socks.'

She shuffled over to the top right drawer of her dresser and shoved things around until she came out with 2 pairs of socks, one bright blue and one bright green. Still singing and bobbing her head with the music, she shuffled back to the bed and stuffed the blue pair into the backpack. She decided she would just ignore Latham standing there in her doorway.

Latham's voice boomed again. 'I said, where do you think you are going?' Sarah lifted her head and looked at him square in the eyes.

'To Sophie's for the weekend, not that it is any of your business!' She was surprised that the words came out of her so easily, and so hoping that they would make him go away. She was determined to enjoy her weekend, and even he was not going to ruin it. He did not belong here. This was her space, and she was not going to let him invade it, physically or mentally. She waited, staring him right in the eyes, for his answer.

His blood boiled under his skin. He had a problem with it. The scheming bitch friend of Sarah's was a thorn in his side. There was no way he was going to let Sarah go spend the weekend with her. Their secret would get out for sure. He just couldn't have that. There was $75,000 riding on it staying a secret. Girls talk.

To make it worse, her behavior seemed to be rubbing off on Sarah. Here he was, standing in the doorway to her bedroom, and instead of being fearful, she was standing up to him, staring him in the face, and asking him what he was doing there. He had more than a problem with it.

When his response did not come soon enough, she went back to singing along with the song that was playing. 'So baby why don't you just fuck off and die..' She glared at him again, as if she was singing it directly to him.

That was the last straw. In an instant, he was inside her room, slamming the door shut behind him. She was still immersed in the lyrics of the song, and not paying attention. In a second, he had her bent over the end of her bed, her arms pinned underneath her, and one strong arm holding her down. The backpack and all of its contents smashed underneath her.

His free hand ripped at her drawstring sweatpants, yanking and pulling one side then the other, frantically, until they were around her knees. He took a deep breath, unbuttoned and unzipped his jeans and let them fall to the floor. He admired his erection. Happy that last night was not a permanent dysfunction. Hard and throbbing, aching to be plunged deep inside the firm, milky white ass in front of him.

His thoughts shifted back and forth between punishing Sarah for how disrespectful she was being and punishing Sophie for stabbing him. He couldn't make up his mind which he was angrier about. It really didn't matter. She was going to pay for all of it.

That thought sent a shiver all the way through him. His erection twitched and he almost came right then and there. He took a deep breath and let the intensity settle slightly. Then he pressed himself firmly against her, his dick pointing at the floor but pressed firmly against her slit.

He writhed and wiggled around against her. He moved his hand up from the middle of her back and gathered a handful of her hair. His other hand supporting his weight. He bent over her to where his mouth was just above her ear. In a growl just slightly louder than a whisper he told her, 'I told you not to go anywhere until you heard from me. You will pay for your disobedience. Maybe this time you will do what you are told. Do you hear me, little cunt?'

She was folded over a bed that hit her just above her knees and with his hand holding a handful of her hair, pulling her head upward, she found it hard to draw a deep breath. The buckles and zippers sticking out all over the place jabbed at her skin. She was certain that her stomach was bleeding in at least one spot where a zipper handle sliced through her skin when he slammed her down on top of it.

She was angry now. He was in her personal space. He barged in on her in her bedroom. She had no idea where her parents were, and he obviously didn't care. She would not be afraid of him anymore. This was her space and although, face down on her bed; she vowed that whatever he did to her in this moment, he would be the one paying. This was the last time.

A whimper was all she could get out in response to his question. He pulled up and back on her hair as he pushed himself upward with his other hand. He held her up just far enough that she could breathe easier.

Her body was tense against him. He enjoyed the feeling of it. It was enough for him. She was in pain and immobilized. The thought of that alone sent another shiver through him. His shaft throbbed and the pressure was building. He would need release soon. He refused to allow it to be over in a simple moment, though. He would wait for the intensity to pass, relishing it more than the orgasm that was to come, eventually.

He held her there, willing his body to calm down. He grabbed and squeezed his erection at the tip, the painful sensation easing its overwhelming need for release. He needed this to last, he needed to be able to take his time, to be as hard as possible, and last as long as possible.

He looked around for a moment. He was plenty hard enough. He could beat the damn thing on top of her dresser right now and the dresser would crack before he did. He needed a way to keep it this way until he was ready. Then he spotted the shoestring dangling from a boot. He reached for it and worked it out of its place. He laid it across the base of his dick and wrapped it around with one hand.

He gathered both ends in his hand and bounced it up and down, rubbing the tip gently against her soft skin. The sensation made him hard as a rock and throbbing again. He shuddered and twisted his hand and tightened the shoelace around it. He rocked his hips backward, lined his erection up with her opening, and thrust forward as hard as he could.

Tears poured from her eyes. Her mouth mimicked a scream, but the only sound was a garbled, throaty growl. She had not been able to take a deep breath for an eternity and the force of his entry felt as though she was being ripped apart in the middle.

He held himself there for a long moment. Every inch of him buried deep inside her, he waited for the throbbing to subside so he could feel her body adjust to him being there. He worked his hips in a circle, slowly swabbing, and feeling for even a twitch of a muscle. Any indication that she was aroused.

He thought he had given her plenty of time to anticipate his entry and for her body to prepare itself. He was surprised that she had not even gotten slightly damp. He knew enough about female anatomy to know that even if they don't want it, their bodies will moisten to reduce friction naturally. She was not at all prepared for this. He smiled. 'Damage.'

He also knew that as hard as he was, no moisture would damage him as well if he kept going. He brought his free hand up to his mouth and spit in it, then he dropped it down and rubbed it against her opening.

A black flash comes barreling into the room. Tank's claws dig into the carpet, stopping him a split second from running head first into Latham's piled up jeans. He looks up and hisses and growls. Latham ignores him. Tank, in a swift and graceful move, leaps onto the bed and then to the top of Latham's head. He wraps himself tightly around Latham's face and bites down hard on his ear. Tank growls loudly as he kicks with his back feet, ripping the skin at the base of Latham's neck.

Latham brings his hands up to his head and tries to dislodge the cat from his face. Its belly is pressed firmly against his nose and mouth, making it hard for him to breathe. He grabs the back legs that are making hamburger meat out of the back of his neck and yanks them away from his head.

Tank's front claws, still clinging on to and biting at the ear, feels himself slipping and digs in even further. Latham lets out a yell. He yanks on the cat until it lets go of his ear and throws him toward the floor. Tank's claws slide smoothly down Latham's face, cutting into the skin like a knife through warm butter.

Tank hits the floor with a thud. Latham, thinking it's over and determined to finish, grabs a hold of Sarah's hips and thrusts into her as hard as he can. He swings his hips backward, readying himself to impale her again. He stops suddenly.

A cat claw is buried in his scrotum and another is now planted deeply into his upper thigh. Latham wasn't sure which hurt more. He screams and pulls away from Sarah completely, cupping his balls with one hand. He smacks at the cat with the other until it lets go of him. He grabs his pants and yanks them up as he runs out the bedroom door.

Chapter 15

Sarah can hear him cussing and yelling all the way down the stairs. She wasn't sure what had happened. She stood there for a full-on minute, ass exposed and the buckle and zipper still digging into her skin. Flaming hot tears stung her cheeks. She pulled up her pants and sat down on her bed when she heard the front door slam. She inhaled deeply and held it for a long moment.

She sat there, tears spilling from her eyes. 'Ahhhhhhhh!' She howled. Her intimate parts burned and every muscle in her body ached. She lifted her shirt to look at the cuts in her stomach. Blood caked and held her shirt to her skin. She peeled it away gently. A small drop developed where the zipper had dug into her the deepest and broken the skin. She jumped up and ran to the bathroom.

She yanked some toilet paper off the roll and applied it to her stomach. She peeled it away from the wound, expecting to see a gaping hole and blood gushing out of it. A tiny drop built up and stopped. She dabbed at it. She stood up and looked at the wounds in the mirror. It wasn't as bad as she thought. There were scrapes, but only the one spot had been deep enough to bleed. She blew out a long breath.

She examined herself in the mirror. Her long, strawberry blonde hair was silky soft and hung just below her shoulders. Her complexion was clear and almost porcelain white, except where she was sun kissed across her nose and cheeks.

She lifted her shirt up over her head and unhooked her bra. She set them on the toilet lid. She went back to looking herself over. Most of the bruising from the other night had diminished. A large patch of yellow-green could still be seen across the tops of her breasts, but it was far less noticeable than the deep purple it has been just a couple days ago.

Fire burned in her chest and hot tears stung her cheeks. She refused to be sad. These were angry tears. Her skin flushed and evaporated the tears almost as quickly as they fell. She stood there, her fists clenched. The question of was it Latham the other night dissolved. There was no more doubt. She swore under her breath.

Questions swirled around in her head and stirred the contents in her stomach. A wave of nausea swept through her. Her body tensed, ready to heave she looked at the toilet. The swirling continued but she refused. She gulped in a deep breath, dropped the bloody toilet paper in the toilet, and walked out of the bathroom.

She sat down on the edge of her bed and Tank came bumbling in. He hopped up on the bed and sat beside her, nudging her arm with his head. She lifted him up to pull him into her lap. His fur was caked and sticky. She pulled her hand away and it was bright red. She scooped him up and rushed into the bathroom. She set him on the counter and held him there with one hand while she filled the sink with water. She slid him into the sink. His claws scratched against the marble surface, but he slid easily.

She washed him off and frantically looked him over for cuts as the water ran red from his fur. 'I'll kill that motherfucker if he's hurt you buddy.'

Tank howled as the water soaked through his fur. His claws dug at the sink surface and he struggled to get away. 'Shhh, I know buddy, it's ok. Be done in a minute.' Sarah stroked his fur and spoke softly to calm him. Tank yowled again but stopped struggling. It was a pleading sound. 'I know buddy. I know.'

Sarah wrapped Tank in a towel when the water was clear again. She carried him to the bed and set him down to really look him over. She felt around through his wet but still thick fur for even the slightest cut or injury. There weren't any.

Sarah laughed out loud. 'You got him good, didn't you? My little hero. She vigorously rubbed him with the towel now that she knew he wasn't injured.

His purr was almost deafening. He seemed proud of himself. He stood up on his back legs and rubbed the top of his head against her chin and neck and pressed his body firmly against hers. She was proud of him too. She put her hand between the top of his head and her chin and scratched between his ears. She loved this cat more than words could ever describe. She had even more reason to now.

She unwrapped him from the towel and let him go. 'I'm still going to kill that bastard. If it's the last thing I do.'

She contemplated sitting back down on the bed and putting her head in her hands. A huge part of her wanted to curl up in a ball and just cry. A loud voice inside of her told her that was a bad idea. If she cried again, he would come back, and she would let him do this to her again. She sucked in a breath.

'That is not going to happen.' She said out loud. She knew that reporting this was what everyone would suggest she do. She knew how that would go though. If he went down for this, she would be going down too. Along with her dad. That was not how she wanted this to end. She would handle this.

'Oh shit! Did Latham kill him?' Her stomach flip-flopped, and her hands flew up to cover her mouth. She had no doubt now. If he could do this, he could easily kill a man. 'Oh my god. She sat down on the edge of her bed. 'Was I the last one to see him alive? The room began to spin.

She steadied herself and sucked in a ragged breath. She had two choices. She could sit here and contemplate and stew about this shit all day, and every day for the rest of her life, or she could get up and go on with her life. Deal with things as they came. Eventually, Latham would pull this again and she would be ready for him. Until then, she had shit to do.

Chapter 16

Sarah pulled into Sophie's driveway at 3:15. She sat in her car for a few minutes trying to pull herself together. Her thoughts raced all the way over here. Latham was the last thing she wanted to be thinking of while she was with her friends. She closed her eyes, inhaled and exhaled slowly several times and cleared her mind.

She repeated to herself, 'I'm excited and looking forward to this weekend. I'm going to have a good time' three times and exhaled as hard as she could. Her stomach was churning but she was determined to have a good time. She yanked the handle of the door and stepped out onto the driveway.

Sophie stepped outside to greet her as she closed the passenger side door and slung a backpack over her shoulder. They hugged each other tightly.

As Sophie pulled out of the hug, she took a step backward and looked Sarah over. 'Are you ok? You look a little green.'

'I'm fine. A little nervous, but I'm fine.' She lied. She was far from fine. Latham had forced himself on her again, but even that was not going to ruin her weekend with these guys. She stuffed her anxiety into her toes, replaced it with a huge smile and a determination to be happy at all cost.

Sophie watched her expression change and knew immediately what it was about. She supported Sarah's courage. She gave her a wink and escorted her inside.

As Sophie entered the house behind Sarah, she closed the front door and yelled into the kitchen. 'I was right, it's Sarah. Come say hello!'

'Be right there!' Todd's voice rang back from the kitchen.

Sarah dropped her purse, keys, and backpack against the wall in the small entry way. Sophie ushered her into the spacious living room. 'What a beautiful place this turned out to be Soph. You guys have done a great job with it.'

'Yeah, it needed a lot of TLC, but it was a steal. We just put the fireplace in a week ago. Come on, I'll show you around.'

Sophie took Sarah on a quick tour. Showing her the back bedroom and bathroom, the second bedroom, but skipped the third bedroom, saying it was still under construction. It really was a much nicer place now that it was all fixed up. 'You guys really did do a great job. It's beautiful!'

They walked in to the kitchen where Todd was slaving over a hot stove. He turned and waved a pot holder in her direction. He wore an apron and had a bandana tied around his head. Sweat was pouring down his face.

'You girls go have a seat. I'll be there in a second.'

'Anything we can do to help?' Sarah asked.

'Nope. I've got this. Thanks. Go. Go. I'll be right there.' He pulled open the oven and smoke billowed up and out of it. 'Shit.'

'He's tossed me out 3 times now. He's pretty serious about doing it himself.' Sophie said as she turned and waited for Sarah to follow her back to the living room. They walked over to the couch and sat down. A moment later, Todd came bounding in. 'Hello Beautiful!' he said as he took her hands, yanked her up off the couch and wrapped her in a hug.

'Well hello to you too, handsome.' Sophie interjected. Knowing full well he wasn't talking to her.

'Not you bitch.' He stuck his tongue out at Sophie. He looked back at Sarah and smiled. 'Welcome to Chateau Todd and Sophie.' He said it with a strange sounding French accent.

Sarah hugged him back. Sophie punched him gently and he recoiled like she had stabbed him. He squealed like a girl. He stepped back and took a long look at Sarah. 'You look amazing. Did you do something different with your hair or something?'

Her anxiety crept up from her toes. *Had he really noticed a change? Would Nate notice it too?* She stuffed it back down again, reminding herself of her promise to herself. He would not interfere with her happiness. 'No, no new do or anything. Just happy to be here. Thanks for the compliment though.'

Todd turned her in a full circle. Something was different. He just didn't know what. 'Nate is going to lose it when he sees you girl. That's all I've heard out of him all week. Is Sarah going to make it? Do you think Sarah will...' Sophie kicked him in the leg. '...enjoy the party...' He looked at Sophie with a convincing wink.

'He is coming then? The last I heard he was going to have to work late.'

'Honey, with you being here, he would happily tell Hank where to shove his two hours of O.T. He ain't missing this.'

A flush of red spread over Sarah's face. She never really tried to hide how happy she was when Nate was around. She couldn't figure out why she was so nervous about it now.

Sophie nodded in agreement. 'Don't worry your pretty little head. He won't be here for another hour or so though, yet. How's about some wine?'

Todd nodded. 'Red or White? I'll get it.'

'Oh yes, definitely some wine. White please?'

'Sure thing milady. Todd winked and turned toward the kitchen. He pranced out of the room, twirling and tossing imaginary glitter into the air around him as he went.

Sarah laughed out loud, and Sophie rolled her eyes. 'I would swear he was a total homo if it weren't for the fact that he has so much sex with me.'

Sarah laughed out loud again. 'What is up with him? I've never seen him act so...gay.'

'Wine. I think. He is excited about tonight. He's done almost all the cooking and the decorating.' She did the air quotes as she said the word. '...for this and has been running around all Martha Stewart-y all day. It's kind of grossing me out a little. She chuckled with a strange look on her face.

'Has he always been this...' she struggled to find the right word. 'Housewife-y?' She laughed as that one came rolling out.

Sophie laughed out loud this time. 'Stop it!' He's excited and happy. I'm not going to rain on his parade.' She yelled into the kitchen. 'Darling, could you bring me my wine on your way back? Please?' She drew out the words in a sultry and almost sophisticated way.

She and Sarah both laughed out loud.

Todd yelled from the kitchen. 'Fuck off bitch. I ain't bringing you shit. I hear you in there talking about me.' His voice got louder as he came into the room carrying three glasses of wine. He handed the white wine to Sarah and one of the reds to Sophie. 'About ten minutes on the bacon wrapped little dicks. Then I can get started on the potatoes and cum.' He kissed Sophie on the top of the head as he stepped past her and squeezed himself between her and the arm of the couch. She slid over a little to give him room.

'That's the Todd I know and love.' Sarah laughed. He wasn't abusive to Sophie, though the way he talked to her sometimes you would have thought so. In truth, Sophie was probably far meaner to him. To Todd, Sophie hung the moon. To her, he was a nice bed warmer, with a nice butt and a dick that would just keep on ticking. This was, and had always been, the way they talk to each other. It really was quite sweet and always entertaining.

'I'm all the Todd you need to know sugar.' He leaned back against the couch and took a long sip of his wine. With his pinky in the air.

Sophie and Sarah both rolled their eyes at that and chuckled. Sophie leaned back against his side as he slid his arm around her waist and pulled her closer to him. They sipped their wine and chatted for a few minutes. Todd jumped up suddenly. 'Back to work. That cum ain't gonna heat itself.' He saluted and then bowed as he excused himself back to the kitchen.

Sophie and Sarah continued to sip their wine and make small talk. Sarah browsed around the room. Taking in all the little details that went into making this a beautiful room. She noticed that there was a table directly behind the couch, a walk space, and then the wall. On the table was a row of picture frames. One of Sophie and Todd together, one of the four of them, and another one of Sophie and Todd. The peculiar part was the small, matching lamps that stood at either end of the table. They were on and shone a soft white glare on the pictures. She caught herself wondering where they were plugged in, being more in the center of the room as they were. She looked over the back of the couch for an outlet but didn't see one. It perplexed her.

She shrugged it off and continued to look around the room. Sophie stopped chatting from time to time and asked Sarah if she was ok and did she need anything. Sarah felt a little tense and a bit out of sorts but was trying hard to keep it tucked away. Apparently, it wasn't working as well as she thought it was.

Sophie finally called her on it. 'What is wrong with you? It's like, you are so uncomfortable and tense? Did something happen?'

Oh geeze. Not now. Don't try to drag this out of me right now. Please? she screamed on the inside. 'Nothing is wrong Soph. I have a lot on my mind and I'm a little anxious about seeing Nate tonight. That's all. It's nothing that won't keep until the weekend is over.'

'Are you sure sweetie? I just want you to have fun but if, given the recent events, needs to be something else, say the word.'

'I'm fine Soph. I am determined to not let things define my life. He doesn't deserve that. So, seriously, I'm fine. You were saying?'

Sophie gave her a hard look. Suddenly, it dawned on her. This was going to be her first encounter with Nate since the rape. Now she completely understood the anxiety that was exuding from her best friend. 'Are you going to tell Nate?'

'Absolutely not! Why would I do that?'

'You don't think he should know?'

Sarah didn't answer right away. Instead, she sat there, silent, as wave after wave of scenarios played out in her mind. Finally, she responded. 'No. He doesn't need to know about it. It would just hurt him. Promise me you won't tell him Soph. I'm fine. Really. I just want to put all of it behind me and get on with my life.'

'Oh Sweetie. You don't just pick up and move on after something like that.'

'I can. I may never be able to forget about it, and I'll never be rid of the filth I feel will never wash off completely, but it doesn't have to, and it will not ruin my life. If Nate knew about it, I don't know what he would do. Things would never be the same though, and I kind of like how they are.'

The doorbell rang. Sarah's eyes grew to the size of dinner plates. Sophie patted her on the leg. 'Relax. I won't tell him anything. I understand your determination and I think it's great. We won't speak of it again.' She hugged Sarah and pulled her to her feet. 'Come, let's go greet him.'

Sarah nodded, and they strolled to the front door arm in arm.

Sophie swung the front door open and yelled so Todd could hear her all the way in the kitchen. 'Well hello Darling! Welcome to Chateau Todd and Sophie. How are you?' she said with a haughty and sophisticated southern drawl.

Nate stepped inside and wrapped his arms around Sophie's waist and lifted her off her feet. 'Hello sweetness.' He kissed her on one cheek and then the other as he spun her in a circle.

Sophie squealed with delight. He set her down gently on the floor as he spoke. 'I'm fantastic milady. How are you?' Sarah stated to laugh as she watched him curtsy, like he was wearing a ball gown.

Sophie replied, 'I'm marvelous Darling. Thank you for asking. Do come in.' The fine Ms. Rosenthal and I were just chatting about you.' She winked at Sarah.

A feeling of betrayal and anger started to boil inside her. She made Sophie promise she wouldn't tell Nate anything and then opened the door and proceeded to nudge him into asking her directly. She glared at Sophie. Sophie took her hand and squeezed it gently. She pulled away from Nate's hug and pushed him gently toward Sarah.

'Oh really?' He cocked his head and looked at Sarah and then back at Sophie. 'All good I hope? He took Sarah's hand and brought it to his lips. He placed gentle kisses across her knuckles.

'Of course, love, we could never talk bad about you.' Sophie winked at Sarah again.

Sarah was a little relieved and grinned from ear to ear as Nate wrapped his arms around her and pulled her in close to him. He leaned in and gave her a long, sultry kiss on the lips.

It was suddenly very hot in the room. She started to sweat and feel a little faint as their lips separated and he smiled at her. She smiled back at him. She had been nervous about seeing him all afternoon. Now that he was here, and she was in his arms, she knew it was going to get a lot easier. She relaxed.

Chapter 17

Nate kept his arm around Sarah as he asked how she was doing. They walked into the living room and sat down on the couch. He never took his hands off her.

Todd came dancing into the room. His arms were in the air and his hips rocked and rotated. A double dip and a turn stopped him facing into the kitchen. He shook and wiggled his ass as he hummed a few lines of the song that only he was hearing. He ran through the steps again and turned. He laughed out loud as he met the stares of the other three people in the room.

He pulled his headphones out of his ears and strode right over to Nate. 'Hey buddy. You made it.' They shook hands old school style, a combination of shakes and high fives, followed by chest bump with pats on the back and a long hug.

'Ok you two, get a room.' Sophie chided.

'Eat a dick bitch.' This is my bro and we will hug all we want to. I'll kiss him too if I want to.' He leaned in with his mouth wide and his tongue wiggling.

Nate took his arm from Sarah's back and leaned in like he was going to engage in this crazy drool exchange with Todd. He backed away at the last second. 'Ha ha. Not a chance bro. Sorry. Boobs, specifically these boobs, win me over every time.' He wrapped his arm back around Sarah and pointed at her chest.

Sarah rolled her eyes and color filled her cheeks. Todd shrugged and walked over to Sophie. 'I love you hunny bunny. He made the wild face with mouth agape and tongue wriggling again. Sophie leaned up and bit the end of his tongue gently. They kissed and made moaning noises.

'Are we like that?' She asked Nate.

'God, I hope not. It's kinda gross.' He laughed.

'Shut up you jealous fuddy duddy. Todd blurted out. 'You wish you had it as good as we do. Ain't that right muffin lips?' He kissed Sophie on the head.

'Absolutely right Buns of Steel!'

Nate made a vomiting gesture and Sarah snorted. Everyone laughed out loud for a full minute.

'Foods about ready. Y'all hungry?'

Everyone nodded and said yes.

'Splendid. Snoocums, want to help me bring stuff out?'

'Absolutely Honey Munch. Nate, be a dear and start the fireplace, would you please?'

'Certainly milady.'

Sophie sauntered into the kitchen. Todd was hot on her heels, patting her on the but as she walked past him.

Nate turned and looked at Sarah. 'Did he just say splendid?'

Sarah chuckled. 'Yeah, he's been in rare form today. It's been quite entertaining. He even pranced earlier.'

'Pranced? Like...' Nate put his hands over his head like a ballerina would do. '...pranced?'

Just then, Sophie came back carrying a tray of bacon wrapped shrimp. 'He sprinkled fairy dust too.'

'Sprinkled fairy...what the hell have you done to my best friend, Sophie?'

Sarah interjected. 'I think all the cooking and decorating has activated his metrosexual gene or something.'

Sophie laughed out loud again. 'I thought the exact same thing! Oh, my god. What if that's exactly what's happened?'

'You have a pretty amazing house husband that you'll never want to get rid of.' Todd spoke in his best Shenaenae voice as he came out of the kitchen carrying a tray, a bowl, and a handful of silverware. 'Why y'all got to be talking shit all the time? Now come on, give momma some love.'

Everyone shot Todd a questioning look. Todd burst into laughter and everyone in the room followed suit. Nate let go of Sarah and walked toward the fireplace. Sarah went to the corner of the room and picked up a blanket. 'Would you like me to spread these out on the floor Soph?'

'Ooh, yeah, that would be great. Thanks.'

Sarah carried the blanket to the center of the room and spread it out on the floor. When the table was full of food, Todd made one more trip to the kitchen with Nate and they brought back 4 glasses of wine. The ladies were busy at the table preparing plates and setting them on the blanket. 'This looks great Todd.' Sarah complimented the chef.

They ate, drank, and played board games until late evening. Sophie and Sarah handled the cleanup in the kitchen while the guys made small talk on the couch. When the last dish was put away and everything was wiped down, the girls joined the guys in the living room.

'I guess the metrosexual gene activation was a temporary thing.' Sophie slung the words jokingly at Todd.

'Shut up and bring that sexy ass over here. No one said everything had to be cleaned up right then.' Sophie walked over and plopped down in Todd's lap. Sarah strode in and sat down next to Nate. He wrapped his arm around her. He kissed the side of her head.

They all sat quietly, listening to the crackle and pop of the flames in the fireplace and the subtle clicking sound of the ceiling fan. They finished their wine slowly and quietly.

Todd and Sophie talked quietly about how nice the evening had been and Nate and Sarah just sat quietly. Their hands intertwined, moving fingers softly over the other's skin. Nate raised her hand to his mouth and planted short, quick kisses all over it.

Chapter 18

It had been a very enjoyable evening. Sarah didn't want it to be over. She had forgotten all about all the troubles plaguing her recently and was just enjoying the moment. She really did enjoy her time with these guys.

She let herself begin to imagine her and Nate in Sophie and Todd's shoes. She pictured herself cooking and cleaning in the kitchen and Nate coming home from work to her. A smile spread across her face.

Sophie shattered the image when she jumped up and announced that they were going to go to bed. She leaned over and hugged Sarah and then Nate. Todd struggled to lift himself up off the couch. Sophie came back over in front of him and offered him her arms. When she had a good grip on his forearms, he bolted to his feet, almost knocking her backwards. He wrapped his arms around her waist and caught her as she stumbled backwards. He lifted her off her feet and squeezed her tight. She wrapped her legs around his middle and laid her head on his shoulder. She waved her fingers and winked at Sarah as he carried her toward the bedroom.

Sarah and Nate waved and said good night to them. Sarah leaned back into Nate and kicked her feet up on the couch. Nate slid down and stretched his legs toward the fireplace. He set his glass down on the table behind him and wrapped his arm around Sarah. 'Hey, where do you suppose those lamps are plugged in at?'

Sarah bolted upright and turned to look at Nate. 'I was wondering the exact same thing earlier.' They both laughed. 'I've had a really great time tonight. The fire, the food, the friends, it's been great.'

'Yeah, the games were great too.' Nate agreed. 'Do you think we will ever have a get together like this one?'

Sarah didn't answer. She didn't really understand the question. 'Do you mean, like a fun and games party, like this again? I'm sure they will come up with some reason to.'

'No. I mean you and me? Do you think that you and I will ever have a place together and invite them over?'

'Oh.' She still wasn't sure how to answer the question. She wasn't sure what he was getting at. 'I suppose one day we might. It doesn't seem like it was that difficult to pull together.' She turned her back to Nate and snuggled up against him. Her thoughts started to race. She had pictured them living together, quite often actually.

'Would you move in with me Sarah?' Nate just blurted the question out. He had been saving up while living with his parents and was finally at the point that he could happily move out and bring Sarah with him.

'Like, with your parents?' She knew that he was still living at home like she was.

'Absolutely not. They love you and all, but I would never move you in there. I mean our own place. I've been working a lot and I'm up for a promotion next month. I've saved up enough for a solid down payment on a house, so I want to know if you would move into a place with me.'

Sarah was shocked. She didn't know what to say. She wouldn't have any problem at all living with Nate. She dreamed about it, often. She had no idea that Nate had been thinking about it too. The question caught her off guard. She was completely dumbfounded.

'Sarah? Did I say something wrong?' The look on Nate's face said it all.

She was struggling to find words. Her life flashed before her eyes but was an imagined one. Her eyes darted back and forth and her mouth hung open, but no words came out.

Nate started to get nervous. If she couldn't come up with a yes or no to this question, how could he ask the next one? He tapped her on the shoulder. 'Sarah, are you ok?'

She shook herself out of her daydream and turned to look at Nate. 'Did you just ask me if I wanted to move in with you?'

Stress washed over Nate's face. 'I did.' He waited for her response but still nothing came. At least he knew she heard the question. Anticipation was killing him. He was sitting on pins and needles and felt like his head was going to explode.

He jumped to his feet and jammed his hand into his pocket. He pulled his hand out and dropped down on one knee. 'Maybe this will help clarify things? Sarah Rosenthal, will you marry me?' He opened the small box he had pulled from his pocket. He pushed it toward her. Right up to an eighth of an inch from her nose.

She backed away just a bit and looked at the box in his hand. There, popping up out of the middle of it was the most beautiful ring she had ever seen. Water filled her eyes and started to stream down her cheeks. *Say something you dote. The man is dying for an answer.* She screamed at herself from the inside. She still couldn't make the word form in her mouth. She nodded her head up and down vigorously.

She leaned in and wrapped her arms around Nate's neck and sobbed.

'Was that a yes?' He was certain that it was, but he wanted to make extra sure.

She nodded her head again against his shoulder. She finally found the words. 'Yes, yes, a thousand times yes.'

Nate laid the ring box down on the couch cushion beside her. He wrapped his arms around her. He kissed her forehead and smoothed her hair. 'Are you ok?'

Sarah backed out of the hug and looked into Nate's eyes. She saw hope teetering on disappointment. He needed an answer that made sense. 'I'm better than ok. You just asked me to marry you. I was shocked and got a little tongue tied.' She wiped at her eyes.

'Ok. I can understand that. I've had a little longer to come to terms with it I suppose. I bought the ring a month ago and had no idea when or how to ask you.' He chuckled awkwardly. 'Do you want the ring?' He held the box up in front of her again.

'Shit! Yes. Of course, I want the ring. I'm sorry. I'm messing this all up.' She took a deep breath and smiled her most sincere smile. 'Yes Nate. I would love to marry you.' Huge tears filled her eyes and rolled down her cheeks again.

Nate pulled the ring out of the box and slid it onto her finger. He was shaking about as badly as she was. He stood up and ran his hands through his hair. On his next breath he yelled. 'She said yes!'

Cheers erupted from the back bedroom. The door flew open and Sophie and Todd came barreling down the hallway. Cheering and whistling all the way. Sophie ran to Sarah and hugged her hard. 'I knew you would say yes.' She hugged her again. She stood up and turned to Nate and hugged him tight, congratulating him. She turned and skipped into the kitchen.

Todd leaned down and hugged and congratulated her too. He stood up and grabbed Nate's hand. He shook it several times. 'I told you she would say yes. Congrats bro!'

Confused and more than a little overwhelmed, Sarah looked at Todd. 'Wait, you guys knew about this? Sophie...', she turned her head toward the kitchen. 'You knew about this?'

Sophie came into the living room carrying a little pink box. She turned to Nate. 'Sit down there next to her Nate.'

Nate nodded and sat down on the couch next to Sarah. He wrapped his arm around her and they looked into each other's eyes. She had never seen him look so happy. They kissed until Todd came bouncing into the room carrying a pie cutter, some plates and silverware, and a camera. Sophie handed Sarah the box. Sarah looked up at her, confused. Sophie nodded. 'Open it.'

Sarah lifted the lid on the box. She tilted her head. 'Awww, it's beautiful. You did plan this.' She leaned toward Nate and showed him what was inside the box. He grinned.

Sarah peeled the sides of the box open and exposed the beautiful white cake inside. It was decorated with red roses and green leaves. On the top, in red icing, it read 'She Said Yes! Congrats Nate and Sarah!' The tears started to fall again. She couldn't remember the last time she felt this loved by her friends. 'So, this whole adult weekend, party thing was planned for this?'

'Pretty much.' Sophie nodded.

Chapter 19

It wasn't long before the cake was gone, and the celebration wound down. Todd and Sophie were off to bed again. Nate led Sarah to the room that had been avoided in the tour earlier and opened the door.

'Constructional mess my ass. You guys are amazing!' Both stood there in awe.

The room was beautiful. There were candles and rose petals everywhere. The astonishing old four post bed was made up with black and purple. Pillows that alternated in tone and texture took up the top half. Real red rose petals had been sprinkled all over it. Nate stayed in the doorway while Sarah stepped in and looked around.

There was an electric fireplace against the wall across from the foot of the bed. Battery operated candles in glass candle holders were topped with tiny bouquets of red roses made of silk ribbon. Rose petals had been sprinkled over the top of them and laid against the wood of the solid mantle top.

The floor had been littered with rose petals. They were cool and squished gently under her feet. The scent of roses permeated the room. She turned her attention to the bed again. She took a few steps and stopped, standing right beside it.

She ran her hand over the fabric of the comforter. It was a very soft and supple black microfiber with squares of silk in varying shades of dark purple. 'My favorite color is purple.'

'Yeah, we know. It's a little presumptive, I know, but they were confident you would accept my proposal, so they did it up nice. Do you like it? '

'Like it? This is incredible! I love it.'

Nate entered the room and started turning on the candles. Sarah watched him move around the room. When Nate turned off the overhead light, Sarah's jaw dropped to the floor. It was a completely different room. The candles lit everything with a yellow orange glow. The electric candles even wiggled and flickered. Shadows bounced and danced on the walls. Sarah was in awe.

Nate closed the bedroom door and walked over to Sarah. He took her hands in his and wrapped them around his neck. He looked into her eyes and moved in to kiss her. He stopped when their lips were about an inch apart and spoke. 'Thank you for making me the happiest man alive.'

'Thank you for making me the happiest woman on the planet.' Their lips met, and they shared a long and passionate kiss. Their hands roamed over and under each other's clothing. Their breathing quickened, and pieces of clothing started melting to the floor.

The heat in the room seemed to rise a hundred degrees for Sarah. The dim and dancing lights in the room made her feel a little dizzy. She clung tighter to Nate.

'What's wrong?'

'I feel a little light headed. Might be I'm just a little overwhelmed by everything that's happened. I'll be alright.'

He turned her gently. Dancing in a slow circle until her back was to the side of the bed. He placed gentle kisses on her neck and shoulders as he eased her a few steps backward. He held her close to him and carefully lowered her to sit on the side of the bed. 'Better?'

She looked up at him and all she could see was the love and care written all over his face. She reached up high around his back and pulled him toward her. 'Much better.' She whispered in his ear.

Nate took her chin in his hand, tilted her head backward and kissed her deeply and passionately. She reveled in the heat and sweetness of it. She released her grasp on him and undid her bra behind her. She pulled her shirt up over her head and undid her pants. She laid back and looked from her jeans to his eyes and back again.

His hands slid gently up her inner thighs to her waistband. She lifted her ass slightly. He slid them down over her hips, struggled at little getting them off her feet as he placed soft kisses on her abdomen. He dropped them on the floor. Never taking his attention from her.

She shifted her weight and spread her legs so that he could stand between them. He pulled off his shirt and tossed it aside. He continued to kiss her as he unfastened his pants and shimmied out of them. He kicked at them until they were lying on the floor next to hers.

He was breathing heavily and so was she. When he was fully naked and standing in front of her, she looked at him and admired every inch of his form. She slid herself backward on the bed and laid back. She stretched and arched her back. He leaned over, placed his hands on her hips and placed little kisses, soft and gently, all over her stomach. She exhaled a quiet moan.

The sound stirred something new in Nate. The temperature spiked, and he started to sweat. His already firm erection started to pulse and ache. He brought his knees up on the bed and positioned himself above her. He was careful not to make any sudden moves or start the end of the game so early. He kissed her again and again. She returned every one of them with heat and passion. Their bodies rocked together in perfect rhythm.

Sarah moaned quietly as his lips moved from her lips to her ear. She nearly melted when he whispered in her ear. 'I love you almost Mrs. Caldwell.' That had such a beautiful ring to it. It escalated her desire for him to a peak. She brought her legs up and wrapped them around him. She feels his want for her pressing hard against her. She shifted beneath him and rocked her hips upward. His tip was now perfectly aligned with her opening.

Nate shivered, even though he was far from being cold. The soft skin of her lips threatened to bring this night to a quick end. He wouldn't have it. He took in a breath and ignored the pain. He forced himself to think of other, less sexual things, just for a few moments. He was frozen in place. Fear of early release plagued him, so he held still and let her do her thing.

She shifted her hips again and pressed them upward. She gasped as the head entered her. It was warm and thick and stretched her opening ever so slightly. She kept pressing and her breath quickened as he moved deeper and deeper inside. She felt his girth against every part of her.

Her soft folds slowly close in around him, pulling him further into her. He gently presses his hips toward the floor. He barely allowed himself to move again. Gently and slowly at first. Her skin slowly swallowing him sent fire through his entire body. His body wanted to thrust hard and deliberate, but he fought the urge and prolonged it.

When she rocked her hips upward and her pubic bone met his, he thought he was going to lose his mind. Everything went blank. He couldn't form a thought. The sense of urgency to be finished he had just a moment ago was gone. He wanted nothing more than to make her happy and enjoy this time with her. He could tell that she wanted him just as much as he wanted her.

He pressed himself against her and slid upward. She moaned and squeezed him with her legs. Pulling him harder against her. She kissed his neck and nibbled on his ear between breaths and soft moans. She ran her hands down his back and squeezed his ass. She pulled him against her. He started to rock himself back and forth. Thrusting on the upstrokes.

He could feel the twitching throbs as her body reached its climax. He nearly came again as she reached her peak and her whole body shuddered. Her insides squeezing and releasing repeatedly. He fought the urge to let himself go again. He shifted his weight to his knees and sat up.

He grabbed her hips and pulled her against him and leaned over her again. Her legs were draped over his arms and he supported his weight on his toes and elbows. He tested his leverage with a few easy thrusts.

The depth of his penetration made her eyes roll back in her head. He had found just the right spot and every thrust against it took her breath away. She tilted her head upward and braced herself against him as he bounced his hips up and down.

Sarah lost control. She held herself open for him and he took her like he owned her. He wrapped his hands over the top of her head and pulled himself into her harder and harder, the sound of their bodies clapping together echoed in the room.

The intensity of Sarah's pleasure reached its peak again. She was about to spill over. She opened her eyes briefly. She expected to see Nate, eyes filled with pleasure and love, staring down at her lovingly. Instead, she saw Latham. His horrible face was grinning back at her. Sweating and grunting as he thrust against her repeatedly. His tongue pushed out to the side of his mouth as he worked to hold her down and take her. She tried to scream.

'Stop.' It was a mere whisper. He kept going. Suddenly, she couldn't breathe. Panic flooded through her and all she wanted to do was get away. She was being raped again, by Latham. She kicked and fought against him. She shifted and squirmed and then, with all her might, she shoved.

Latham flew backward off the bed and into the wall behind him. She screamed at him. 'I said stop dammit!' She sat up. Nathan rushed back to her. Huge tears streamed down her face.

'Did I hurt you? Baby I'm so sorry. You know I would never try to hurt you. I'm so sorry.' He tried to console and talk to her. She pushed him away. She stood up and got dressed. Nate didn't understand what was happening. He just knew that she was hurt and he had to fix it. 'Baby. You gotta talk to me.' She pushed past him and out of the room without saying a word.

Nate followed her, saying whatever he could think of to get her to stop and turn to look at him. She picked up her purse, backpack, and keys, and went out the front door, slamming it shut behind her. Nate watched her through the window as she got into her car, backed out of the driveway, and sped off.

Nate turned around and sprinted back to the bedroom. He ran into Sophie in the hallway. After they collided, Sophie leaned to her right and flipped on the light switch. She stood there and looked at Nate. His sweat drenched body glistening in the hall light. Sophie kept her eyes on his. 'Something wrong?'

Nate covered himself with his hands. 'It's Sarah. She just stormed out, crying.'

'Did you guys have a fight?' The question didn't make any sense in her own head even as she asked it.

He shot her a funny glance. 'Does it look like we had a fight?'

She looked him over and covered her mouth with her hand. 'Oh shit. I'm so sorry.'

'What? What's wrong?' He looked down at himself. The way she said that made him think he was covered in blood or something. He looked himself over. He wasn't covered in anything but sweat and shame.

'Get dressed and meet me in the kitchen. We need to talk.'

'Just spill it Sophie.'

'Just get dressed. You want to be sitting down and probably have a drink in your hand for this.'

'Tell me what is wrong Sophie. What the hell happened?'

'I...I can't talk to you about this like...' she pointed to his lower body 'like that. Please get dressed and meet me in the kitchen?'

Nate growled and stomped into the bedroom. He pulled on his pants and grabbed his shirt. He stormed into the kitchen. Sophie was pouring herself and Nate a glass of wine. Todd was sitting at the dining room table, barely awake. Sophie slid Nate's glass toward him across the high counter. She stood at the sink and took a long sip of hers. Nate sat down on a stool and took his drink.

Chapter 20

'**A**lright, spill' Sophie sucked in a breath. 'I am so sorry about this Nate. She made me promise not to tell you.' She scratched her head and then rubbed her eye. She couldn't believe she was about to betray Sarah's trust. He needed to know what had happened though. This might change things, but he needed to know that the problem wasn't him.

'Not to tell me what, Sophie?'

Sophie took another long sip of her wine. She searched her brain for a gentle way to tell him. There really wasn't one. She didn't want to beat around the bush and leave him with more questions than answers. She looked over at Todd. He would be no help in this situation. He didn't know what had happened either. She looked back at Nate. 'There's no easy way to say this Nate. She was raped recently.'

'She was...what?' The word refused to register in his brain. He couldn't believe it. 'When? Who?'

'Monday night, on her way home from Bull Shots.'

Nate sat there, staring at Sophie's face. Waiting for an expression that indicated she was kidding. It never came.

'Are you fucking serious? Why didn't you tell me? Why didn't she tell me?' Nate looked down at the floor between his feet.

'She was dealing with it. She said she could handle it. She said she didn't want you to know because you didn't deserve to be hurt.'

'What does that mean?'

'I think she feels guilty about it and thinks that you would feel differently about her and your relationship.'

'I see.' He sat quietly for a long moment. 'No. Actually. I don't see. How does that at all explain what just happened?'

'I don't know. What just happened?'

'I have no idea. Things were fine. We were happy, enjoying each other, and then she just shoved me into the wall. Then she leaves crying. I tried to talk to her. She ignored me. I tried to hug her. She shoved me away and stormed out the door.'

'Were you guys about to...you know?'

Nate looked her dead in the face. 'About to? No. We were...right... in the middle of it.'

'Wow. She was able to get that far? Good for her!'

'What do you mean get that far and good for her?'

'She was raped, less than a week ago, Nate. Beaten and violated in the worst possible way. Women don't just suddenly bounce back to 100%, no

---

69

matter how determined they are. Most of them don't have sex again for months or even years.'

'It was good that she was able to get back on the metaphorical horse again so quickly.' Todd chimed in with his eyes still closed.

'Ok. Let me wrap my head around this. She was raped? Monday night? On her way home from...was it that weird guy that showed up that night? She knew he was there for her. Oh god, I knew I should have followed her home that night.'

'Yeah. She's pretty sure it was him. She said she never saw his face, but she's pretty certain that it was Latham.'

'You know his name? That means he's in jail, right? She's no longer in danger?'

'Um, no he's not in jail. I met him when I was at her house the other night. A real piece of shit if you ask me. She didn't report it. No matter how much I tried to convince her, she refused.'

'What? Why would she do that?'

'Same reason a lot of women don't. Fear and guilt. In her case though, I think he threatened her family and I think that she really and truly believes that she can just move on and eventually forget about it. She refuses to let him ruin her life. She was pounding on him pretty good when I showed up.'

'Pounding on him? Soph?'

'He had just shown up when I got there. She was angry and was punching him in the chest when I walked up. I didn't know who he was, but I told him I didn't know what was going on, but that he should probably leave before somebody got hurt.'

'What did he do?'

'He left.'

'And then?'

'And then, we went to her room and she told me what happened. She was bruised all over Nate. Her chest looked...'She looked at Nate and watched as anger boiled inside him. 'I'm sorry. You don't need details. She was just really shaken up and angry.'

'So what do we know about this guy? Why would she not report it? I just don't understand.'

'I honestly don't know. She made all the normal excuses but I also found out that he is a friend of her dad's or something. Since she hadn't seen his face when it happened, she didn't want to accuse him and be wrong.'

'Who do you think it could have been?'

'After meeting the guy...' Sophie thought back to their encounter in the guest house later that night. A chill crept up her spine. 'Yeah, he's plenty capable and if I had to guess, I'd say it was him.'

'Jesus fucking Christ that's awful! And you met him after the fact? He showed up at her house afterward?'

'Yeah, he showed up. He walked in like he owned the place. She was punching and screaming at him. I stayed with her that night.'

'You stayed with her that night? That's good.'

'Well I stayed in the guest house, but yeah.' There was a brief pause before the rest of her answer. She had called me early that day and said she needed to talk. I showed up and he was there.'

'So he didn't leave right away?'

'No. He went on into her dad's study.'

'He did leave eventually though?'

'Yeah. I think he was sticking around to make sure she didn't tell me anything. When I told her that I was going to stay in the guest house that night, he left.'

'He didn't come back later?'

She didn't hesitate to answer the question. 'No. He didn't come back and bother her anymore.'

'You're sure?'

'I'm sure.' Sophie was about to back herself into a corner. The last thing she wanted to do was tell him how she had set herself up for him to come back later and have him attack her. Nor did she want to tell him that he had come back, attacked her, and ended up being on the receiving end of her blade.

'So you probably stopped it from happening again.'

'I guess you could say that.' The sickening feeling threatened to overwhelm her. 'I think that there is more to the story than that but she wouldn't say any more about it. She just insisted that her dad didn't deserve to go down like that.'

'Down like what?'

'I really don't know. She wouldn't say.'

Nate ran his hands through his hair a couple of times. He looked Sophie in the eye for a brief moment. 'I have to go.' In a flash, he was on his feet and out the door.

Sophie ran after him. 'Where are you going?'

'To take care of my future wife!' was the last thing he said before he pulled the car door closed and peeled out of the driveway.

'Shit!' Sophie cursed and then ran back inside. Todd was already in the bedroom.

Chapter 21

Sophie thought Todd has just gone back to bed. She rushed into the room and was surprised when she found him in the closet. He was shifting through her clothes and came out with a pair of jeans and one of her favorite tops draped over his arm.

'I figured you would be getting dressed and going after them, and you would need these.'

'You aren't coming?'

'Why would I? He's taking care of his woman. I would never try to talk him out of that.'

'I have to go make sure she is alright.'

'I know.' He kissed her on the cheek. 'I'd just be in the way. She talks to you more openly when I'm not around. So, go take care of her. I'm drunk anyway and would just make a fool of myself.'

Sophie grabbed and squeezed both of his hands as she kissed him on the cheek. 'You're always such a thoughtful and understanding wife.' She kissed him again.

'Shut up and get going before I decide that you need punishing for that statement and throw you back in this bed.' The look on his face was quite serious.

'Yes daddy." She made a quick pouty face and then smiled. She changed out of her pajamas quickly and into the clothes he had picked out for her.

Todd lay back in the bed and watched her change. He shifted the covers and her eyes grew as she saw his erection lift the covers and form a tent over his middle. She cocked her head to the side. 'Babe! Really?'

'What can I say? You going to play the night in shining armor is a turn on.' A sly grin spread over his face.

'The wind is a turn on for you.' She sat down on the edge of the bed beside him and leaned over to kiss him. He allowed a quick peck but stopped her from going any further. His will power would only stretch so far.

'Go. On. This will be here when you get back.' He kissed her on the forehead. 'She needs you more than I do right now.'

Sophie nodded and headed out the door.

Chapter 22

Sarah pulled into her driveway, threw the car in park, and slammed the car door and stormed into the house. She slammed the front door behind her so hard the windows rattled. Her dad stepped out of the study.

'What the hell Sarah? Everything alright?'

'No! Everything is not alright. You can talk to Latham about that though.' She blew past him like he wasn't standing there. She stomped into the kitchen sink and filled a glass with water. She grabbed some pain relievers from the cabinet. She popped three of them into her mouth and washed them down in three large gulps.

She was breathing heavily when she set the glass back in the dishrack. Her stomach churned and gurgled. She turned and dashed back toward the stairs and took them three at a time all the way up. She bolted through her bedroom door and into the bathroom.

She barely made it to the toilet. Heaving the contents of her stomach into the bowl. She wretched until her eyes watered, and her lungs burned for air. She gasped and tried to suck in a breath. It was like breathing through a straw for a moment. She heaved again. When she was finally able to breathe again, she sat down beside the toilet and savored the ability.

She heard the doorbell ring. It was one am. She figured it was Nate. She knew Nate wouldn't just leave things the way they were. He loved her more than that, she knew it. She wasn't quite ready to face him just yet and hoped that her dad would answer and detain him with questions about her behavior. He had a knack for that.

She rinsed her mouth several times with water, and then with mouthwash. She moved into her bedroom and changed her clothes. She was feeling a bit sorry for herself and childish, so she dressed accordingly. Her favorite fuzzy pajamas were a soft baby blue and had yellow rubber ducks stamped all over them. The tank top was the same color blue. She turned toward her bed and heard it calling to her. She ignored it.

She wanted to know for sure that the midnight visitor was Nate and not another surprise visit from Latham. He didn't usually ring the doorbell though. She slipped her feet into her fuzzy slippers and strode down the stairs. Whoever it was, her dad had already escorted them into his office. She could hear mumbled voices coming from the study.

Chapter 23

Jacob answered the front door confused, and now concerned. 'Nathan!' He reached out the door and shook Nate's hand. 'How are you? Sarah just got home a few minutes ago. She didn't seem very happy. Is everything ok?'

Nate returned the handshake and shook his head. 'No sir, I'm afraid everything is not ok. Can we talk?'

He was trying to contain his all-out anger and refrain from lashing out at a man he's respected and admired for a while now. He couldn't control the flaring of his nostrils or the anger that burned white hot in his eyes.

Jacob was even more confused now. He made a valiant effort to not get involved in the disputes between the two of them in the past. He really had no idea how to advise them now though. With his marriage on the fritz and all. All he could do was listen and go from there. 'Sure son. Come on in. We can talk in the study.' He stepped aside and ushered Nate in.

Nate nodded and strode past Jacob toward the study. He looked up toward the top of the stairs where he knew Sarah's room to be. He was half-hoping he would see Sarah standing there, glaring down at him. She wasn't. It was dark and not a drop of light spilled from under her bedroom door.

He knew she had made it home. Her car was in the driveway and was not damaged at all. He'd checked carefully before he rang the doorbell. He continued toward the study.

'Do you want her to come down and we can deal with this together?'

'No sir, this part I need to discuss with you, just you.' The tone of his voice was ominous.

Jacob was completely confused now. He knew that Nate had been planning to propose this weekend. He had come to him three weeks ago, showed him the ring, and asked for his blessing. It was the sweetest thing. He couldn't imagine that she would say no. 'So, I take things didn't go as planned?' He followed Nate into the study, pulling the door mostly closed behind him.

Nate didn't respond right away. He entered the room and headed toward the large upholstered chair that sat on the client side of Jacob's desk. He recalled how intimidating this room felt the first time he stepped into it. Since then, he and Jacob had gotten to know each other. It wasn't so scary anymore.

Jacob stepped around to the CEO side of the desk and motioned for Nate to take a seat. Sarah and Nate were happily in love and were perfect for each other. He couldn't for the life of him imagine why she would have said no. He sat down and looked up at Nate.

Nate glared at him. He couldn't help it. He had to know that Jacob was not behind Sarah's rape. He had to be certain that Jacob had nothing to do with it. He just spit it out. 'Do you know a guy by the name of Latham sir?' Anger flashed in his eyes like lightning.

Jacob's level of confusion doubled. 'What could he possibly have to do with their problems? He had been a thorn in Jacob's side for a while now, showing up out of the blue from time to time, but Jacob had a lot going on and it was good to have him around offering to help. He couldn't for the life of him think of why Nate would be inquiring about him. They had no reason to interact that he could think of.

He answered cautiously. 'I do know a Latham. He's an associate of mine. Why?'

Nate used every ounce of his will to not reach across the desk and strangle the man sitting in front of him. Sophie's story about this guy had merit. It wasn't enough to convict him though. Yet. He had known Jacob and the rest of the family for a while now and he just couldn't fathom Jacob being able to put someone up to something like that. Especially not to Sarah. She was his pride and joy. Nate felt lucky that he could be with her.

'Have you noticed anything strange about Sarah lately?'

Jacob recalled the last few times he had seen and interacted with Sarah. She had grown up beautifully. She was kind and courageous and had become quite independent. He hadn't noticed anything strange except that he had not seen much of her at all. Tonight, was the longest conversation they'd had in weeks. I can't say that I have, until tonight. I've never seen her come storming in like she did tonight. She could throw some hellacious fits when she was younger, but she's grown up a lot since then. What's this all about?'

'I...I just need answers sir.' Nate stared at him hard.

'Oh. Hold on. Let's start at the beginning then. I am happy to tell you what I know, if it's anything, but I need to understand. Tonight, was the night you were supposed to propose, was it not?' Jacob assumed that things had not gone as they both thought they would. He was saddened for the young man. He stood up and turned toward the liquor cabinet to pour him a drink.

Nate needed to calm down. He needed answers, but he also needed a clear head. The conflict between the implication that Jacob played a role in hurting Sarah and the man he knew Jacob to be were not playing well with his mind or his heart. He ran his hand through his hair and sucked in a breath. He exhaled slowly before speaking. 'Yes sir, it was, and she said yes.'

Jacob set the bottle down and turned to look at Nate. 'She said yes, and you are fighting? You should be celebrating and consummating, not sitting here in my office, fighting. What happened?'

'We aren't fighting sir. She's a bit freaked out, but we aren't fighting.'

'Freaked out about what?' His confusion growing substantially, he decided to just pour the drinks and hear the whole story.

'That's what I'm trying to find out sir. See, things were going great. We had a lot of fun with Sophie and Todd until they went to bed. I proposed. She was a lot more shocked than I expected, but she said yes. Sophie and Todd came out and we all celebrated. With cake and everything. It was great. We went to bed and things were all done up nice and romantic like and...' He paused. Unsure of how much detail to tell her father. He did value his life and could only imagine how infuriated he would be hearing about some guy 'giving the goods' to his own daughter someday.

'And?' Jacob ignored the nervous undertone in Nate's voice and the uncomfortable pause. This was not easy for him to hear, but he knew Nate well enough to know that he wouldn't mention it if it wasn't important. 'Go ahead. Did you guys seal the deal or not?'

'Well, we started to. We were right in the middle of it and she freaked out. She shoved me into the wall, yelled at me to get away from her, got dressed and stormed out.'

'Why would she do that?'

'Well, I talked with Sophie before I came after her. She said that this guy Latham raped her sir.'

'He what?' Jacob knew Latham to be a lot of ugly things, but a rapist; he had to think about that for a moment. He eyed the gun that sat behind the crystal decanter and tumblers. He would destroy Latham if a word of this was true.

'He showed up at the pool hall Monday night and Sarah started acting weird.'

'Weird how?'

'Well, like she knew him and knew he was there for her. She wanted nothing to do with him, so Sophie and a couple of her bouncers ran him off.'

'He showed up at the pool hall looking for her?'

'Yes sir. Or well, she assumed so. He wouldn't have belonged there otherwise. Then Sophie said that she showed up her a few days later and Latham was here. Sarah was yelling at him and punching him. She was pretty banged up from what Sophie said. Sophie stayed in the guest house that night. She tried to talk Sarah into reporting it, but she just wouldn't.'

'She didn't report it? Why would she not do that immediately? Why would she not come to me at the very least.'

'Sophie said something about she couldn't because you didn't deserve to go down like that. That's why I'm here sir. To find out what you had to do with it. I couldn't believe it sir. It's eating me up to be here even thinking about confronting you. I respect you sir, but your job, the people you could have...' His voice trailed off.

Jacob turned as white as the clouds on a sunny day. His tongue seemed to swell in his throat and dry out. He tried to clear his throat. The images of Derrick Murphy, standing in front of him, the words coming out of his mouth, and then him lying on the floor, limp, flashed through his mind. His stomach sank. 'When was she raped?'

'On Monday night, sir.'

'Is she certain that it was Latham?' His hand squeezed on the handle of the gun, still in the cabinet.

'No sir. According to Sophie, when she met him she knew that he was capable. Sarah was pretty certain, but she never actually saw his face that night.'

Jacob started to sweat. He couldn't believe that Latham would do something like that. Why would he. He had confided in him with a terrible secret, why would he betray him like that? He couldn't disbelieve his daughter either though. Latham had become a lot more present since the incident, but as he promised, they had not spoken a single word about it. Surely, he hadn't dragged Sarah into his mess. She was never supposed to know.

'Based on her behavior tonight sir, it's a reasonable assumption. The only missing piece is why he would do it. When Sophie told me he was an associate of yours...'

'You had to assume I had something to do with it.' Jacob turned around to face Nate. His head was low, and his outstretched hand was shaking. The gun in it was almost heavier than he had the strength to hold now. Nate recognized the gun and immediately jumped up out of his seat and stepped around behind the chair. 'What are you doing sir?'

Sarah let out a loud gasp when she saw the shiny metal of the gun in her father's hand. She covered her mouth and darted back up the stairs. Jacob and Nate both heard the gasp from the hallway. Nate turned and saw Sarah's backside dart away.

Jacob jumped out of his skin. The gun fell from his hand and landed on the desk with a loud bang.

The bullet in the chamber found a safe place to land deep in Jacob's chest. He stood there for a moment, wide eyed and still, as the realization hit him. He fell slowly and was gone before he landed on the floor with a thud.

Nate turned wide eyed at Jacob. He watched him fall to the floor. 'Oh sir.' He wasn't sure what to do now. He could only see Sarah frantic and alone. He darted out the door and up the stairs after her.

Chapter 24

Sarah listened to the muffled voices for a few moments from the third step. When she was certain that the voices belonged to Jacob and Nate, she crept down the last few steps and approached the slightly open study door.

She hadn't heard a word either of them had said well enough at this point to know what they were discussing. She watched and listened more closely now. Tears filled her eyes as she heard Nate reveal that she had been raped and anger boiled inside her. She couldn't believe that her best friend betrayed her like this, but under the circumstances, she guessed she understood. Here Nate was now, trying to be a hero. She really loved this guy.

She watched as her dad's back was turned to the liquor cabinet and the conversation continued. Shame and guilt played an agonizing game of tag throughout her body. She was tired and angry and sick all at the same time. She didn't want to hear anymore. As she was about to turn and head back upstairs, Jacob turned around.

A shiny metal object shook in his hand. From her vantage point, it was pointed right at Nate. She watched him duck behind the huge upholstered chair and knew. It was the gun. She gasped and bolted up the stairs.

She reached the third step again and heard a loud bang. She covered her mouth and stifled a scream. She heard the study door creak open behind her. She darted up the remaining steps. When she reached the top, she grabbed the nearest thing to her and waited for Jacob to come and take care of her next.

When the footsteps reached the top of the stairs, she panicked. She turned her back to the stairway and thrust the pointed end of the umbrella behind her as hard as she could and stood there. Frozen.

Nate called her name as the sharp point of the umbrella punctured his chest wall. He brought his arms up and wrapped both hands around the protrusion he was now impaled by. 'Sarah.'

Sarah jerked her head around with tears spilling from her eyes. 'Nate!' She yelled. She let the umbrella go and turned toward him. 'Oh fuck! Nate! What have I done?'

'Sarah. I'm ok.' He choked as he looked downward. Blood splattered across his chest.

'Oh god! Nate! What are you doing here? Oh god. Nate, baby please don't die! What have I done? Oh Jesus. Nate!'

Nate fell to his knees. His eyes were wide and glossy, staring straight ahead. Sarah fell with him. She wrapped her arms around him. She didn't know what to do. 'Oh god Nate. What do I do?' She reached for the umbrella to pull it out. Nate put his hand on hers to stop her. He knew that if she pulled it out, he would be dead in a second. 'Leave it. It's fine.' He wrapped his hands around her face and placed a kiss on her forehead. 'I love you Sarah.'

She buried her face in his neck. 'I'm so sorry Nate. I'm so sorry!'

He shushed her and held her tightly for his last few breaths.

Sarah felt his body go limp and wailed. 'Naaaaaaate!!!!' She sobbed as she stroked his hair. Still sitting there on their knees. She slowly pulled away from and lowered him to the floor with his head in her lap. She gently kissed the top of his head several times and rocked him as she whispered 'I love you. I'm so sorry' over and over again. He just stared up at her. Lifeless.

Chapter 25

Nate was gone. She was rocking and consoling a dead body. 'Shit!' She gently lifted Nate's head and slipped out from beneath him. She lowered his head as softly as she could and closed his eyes. She stood up and looked down at him. He looked like he was sleeping. Except there was an umbrella sticking out of his chest. Blood had started to pool around it, a thick sticky black circle spread out from it and spilled down his sides. Tears rolled from her eyes.

The doorbell rang. Her head snapped around and she glared down at the front door. She expected it to be Latham. 'Speak of the devil and he will come.' She said to herself. She clomped down the stairs, rage boiling inside her. The doorbell rang again. 'I'm coming asshole!' When she got to the door, she swung it open like wonder woman. She was going to kill him.

She was shocked to find Sophie standing there in front of her. Panic washed through her.

'Soph. What are you doing here?'

Sophie seemed to be in her own kind of panic. The words spilled out of her at a hundred miles an hour and were mumbled. 'Well, you left in a huff... Nate was all upset...The poor boy was so dumbfounded...I gave him a glass of wine...told him about that Latham guy...he left... I don't know where he is now. I didn't mean to. I didn't know what else to do. I'm so sorry Sarah.' She sounded as befuddled as Sarah felt.

'Ok. Wait. Come on in the kitchen and sit down. Then you can start at the beginning.' They walked into the kitchen. Sarah turned on the cold water and washed a few smears of blood off her hands. She noticed them in the light of the entry way. She stood upright and looked herself over. She wasn't covered.

Sophie took a seat and continued. 'He was so upset. Confused really. You bolted on him so quickly and he had no idea why. I couldn't leave him believing it was his fault Sarah, that's just not right. You should have told him. What if he is out there right now trying to hunt Latham down and kill him?'

'He's not. Wait! You told him?' She feigned panic over the news. It was easy since there were two dead bodies in the house. She assumed that since it was Nate that chased her up the stairs that Jacob was dead too. Sarah had no idea what to do.

'I had to. If you had seen his face Sarah. He was broken. No idea what had happened, or why.'

'So, what made you think he was going after Latham?'

'He was so pissed off Sarah. I don't know what he was going to do. Wait. Was that his car on the street out front? He came here?'

Sarah flopped down in the chair next to Sophie. Her adrenaline level dropped suddenly, and she felt weak and tired. It was right about then that the front door opened and closed. The sound of heels clacking on the tile in the entry way divulged who had entered.

Olivia came strolling into the kitchen. She went straight to the sink and grabbed a glass and turned toward the fridge. When she looked up and saw Sarah and Sophie sitting at the table she jumped. 'Oh. Haaay Sarah. What are you doing here? I thought you were staying at the red headed bimbo's hou...' She stopped herself from finishing the sentence as she realized that Sophie was sitting there with her. 'Oh. I'm sorry. I didn't mean...'

'Jesus mom. Drunk again?' She grabbed Sophie by the arm and pulled her toward the basement stairs. 'Come on Sophie, you don't need to be subjected to her hatefulness.'

Sophie's head perked up. She had not heard what Olivia said or the reason for them going to the basement. The next thing she knew she was being grabbed by the arm and dragged down the basement steps.

When they got to the bottom of the stairs, Sarah found the light switch and flipped it on. The room lit up, but barely. It was more of a storage room for her parents and was the same for her grandparents before them. Old farming tools still hung from racks on the ceiling held up by chains.

'Ok Soph. Listen to me. I've got something that I need to take care of upstairs. I want to talk to you about this but I really need you to stay right here until I get back.'

Sophie leaned against the table behind her. 'Wait? Here? In the basement? What's going on Sarah?'

'I don't really know yet Soph. Nate was here with my dad and I was coming down to eaves drop when you showed up.' She lied. 'Now my mom's here and drunk...Jesus...Just wait here. Please?'

'Oh, he's here? Whew! Good. Wait. Why did he come here?'

'Just wait here Soph. I'll explain everything in a little bit.' Sarah stepped back and looked at Sophie. A pleading look on her face.

Sophie wasn't going to let this go. She knew something was up and she refused to leave her best friend to deal with it alone. That and this old basement gave her the creeps. 'No. I will not. Something is up and you are going to tell me about it or I am going back upstairs with you.' She stood up from her lean against the table and was about to move toward Sarah.

There was an audible cracking sound inside Sarah's head. Her pleading look morphed into something else. Something dark and angry. Sophie noticed it immediately, but still a moment too late. Sarah lunged at her. Shoving her backward against the table again. She reached down beside the table and pulled a chain with an old shackle on the end of it and yanked Sophie's arm toward it.

'What the hell are you doing Sarah?' She struggled against Sarah. The grip Sarah had on her was not painful, but it was stronger than she anticipated. Sarah had the shackle wrapped around Sophie's wrist in a split second. Sarah backed away and glared at Sophie. 'Just...wait!'

Sarah bolted toward the stairs. She turned and looked at Sophie once more and then darted and was gone.

Chapter 26

Olivia was still in the kitchen when Sarah reached the top of the basement steps. She was sitting at the dining room table with her head in her hands.

She could really care less about her mom's problems at that moment. With Nate dead upstairs and her dad dead or dying in his study, she really didn't have time to sit and listen to her mom go on about how some department store didn't have the exact shoes she was looking for. She took a deep breath and stepped into the kitchen anyway.

She made her way to the fridge, trying to act like nothing was wrong. She looked her mom over. Her head was down, her hair disheveled, tears in her eyes. This was a shock to Sarah. Her mother never cried about anything. She was always either staunch and proper or mean and intoxicated. This was odd. 'Everything ok, mom?'

Olivia rubbed at her eyes and temples. 'No. Not really. I got served divorce papers at work today.'

'Divorce papers? From dad?'

'Nope. The postman. Of course, from your dad. Use your head Sarah!'

Sarah didn't know what to say. She was used to her mom's belittling and would usually shrug it off. This time though, it grated against her already raw nerves. She wanted to pour salt in the obvious wound. 'So, he's cutting you off, huh? Seems fitting.' She smirked at the idea of it and what it had to be doing to her mother's insides.

Olivia shook her head and got up from the table. She went to the cabinet above the sink to grab and swallow a handful of pain relievers. Olivia changes the subject. 'So, aren't you supposed to be at what's her names house, getting proposed to?'

'You knew about that too?' Surprise spread over Sarah's face. 'Yeah. I was. He did. I said yes.' She knew her mom had an attention span of about three words if the subject was not about her. She left it at that.

Olivia nodded. 'Don't you think you should tell him about Latham?'

'What about Latham?'

'You know. That you and him are, what are they calling it these days, bumping uglies?'

Anger flashed in Sarah's eyes. She stood there with her jaw gaping. 'What did you say?' Her attitude changed abruptly. She went from slightly worried about her mother's mental state to enraged in a flash. Did she just hear her mom say that she knew Latham had raped her?

'I don't care who you have sex with Sarah. Nate's a good boy though. You should be honest with him about it.'

'Who I have...how do you even know I'm having sex with anyone?'

'Yesterday morning. I came out of my room and there you guys were door wide open, like it was free for the entire world to see.'

'You saw him raping me?'

'Raping you? Get real Sarah. Even you couldn't stoop that low. Accusing someone of rape. There was no rape from what I could see.' The smugness in her voice was bone chilling.

'You bitch!' Sarah spit the words out at her mom like they were acid. Sarah glared at her. She couldn't believe what she was hearing.

'Hey now. You will not speak to me that way. I'm your mother and you will respect...'

Sarah stormed up to her mother and cut her off. 'I will not! You knew what he was doing to me and you did nothing! What the hell kind of mother are you?'

'What he was doing to you? Well I wasn't being a voyeur. I just happened to walk out and see you...and him...stuck together. You're an adult, so is he...what was I supposed to think? How would I have known you weren't enjoying it?'

'Enjoying it? Enj...I can't believe that you would think for a second that that horrible beast of a man would be doing anything to me that I could enjoy!' Just the sound of it was like a lemon being placed in the back of her throat. Spittle flew from her mouth and sprayed Olivia in the face.

Olivia raised her hand back to slap her daughter. Already unsteady and with the room spinning, she awkwardly swung her arm toward Sarah's face. Sarah caught her mother's hand mid swing. She would not stand there and be slapped by the woman that ignored her anguish and accused her of enjoying it. Her mother or not.

Olivia had put everything she had into her swing. The motion threw her forward and she stumbled when Sarah caught her by the arm. She fell backwards, pulling Sarah to the floor with her. Olivia's head hit the marble floor hard, splitting her skull and knocking her unconscious.

Sarah failed to notice that the force of the fall had caused her mother to black out. She didn't really care. Something inside her had completely shifted. She was no longer Sarah, the Senator's daughter. She was now just a ball of fire, fueled by rage, hatred, and resentment.

Images of Nate lying on the floor, a hole in his midsection, lifeless and alone flashed through her mind. She wanted him to be alive still, for them to get married and live happily ever after. That was gone now though. It was replaced by images of that night, slammed into the front end of a truck and rent from one end to the other. She remembered that fire all too clearly.

She screamed at her mother. 'You bitch. How could you just walk away when he was doing that to me? You aren't a mother, you are a drunken whore and I hate you!' She pounded out every syllable on Olivia's face. Her face suddenly morphed right before Sarah's eyes. Suddenly, it was Latham there beneath her. Laughing.

She poked her fingers into Olivia's eyes and lifted and pounded her head into the cold stone floor. Over and over again. She ignored the blood that spattered in every direction. It's sticky warm wetness spraying her in the face with each slam. She had to stop. She willed herself to stop, but it wasn't her in control anymore.

Her phone buzzed in her pocket. The bashing stopped and she started to sob. Tears streaked down her cheeks. She looked around the room. Blood had splattered everywhere. The stark white cabinets had specks of red all over them. She looked down at her mother and watched through tear filled eyes as blood began to pool around her head. Sarah put her hands to her mouth. They were soaked in her mother's blood.

She stood up and heaved into the sink. Having emptied all the solid contents of her stomach earlier, it was just foamy and thick acid. It burned her throat and nose.

She turned on the faucet and drank directly from it. Swishing the cold water around in her mouth in an attempt to neutralize the taste and burn. It was futile. She spit the water into the sink. She ran her hands under the water, wringing them together until the water flowed clear. Her phone buzzed again.

She dried her hands on the towel on the counter and yanked her phone out of her pocket without a second thought. 'Hey.' She answered.

'I'm in the guest house. We have a problem.'

She rolled her eyes. Seeing her mother's limp body on the floor in front of her as they rolled downward. She turned toward the study. 'Damnit Latham, I really don't have time for your bullshit right now.' She hung up the phone. If there was ever not a good time, this was it. She needed to go check on her dad. She wanted to get back to Nate and Sophie was still in the basement. All she wanted to do was get back to Nate.

Her phone buzzed again. She tapped the power button to silence the call. She walked slowly out of the kitchen and through the entryway to the door of the study. It was wide open. She stood in the doorway, frozen. Afraid to go in.

Her phone buzzed in her hand. She slid her finger across the screen. 'I told you now is not a good time.'

'I don't care if it's not a good time. Get your ass to the guest house!' Latham hung up this time.

His words cut right through her. She chucked her phone at the wall across the room. She watched as it shattered into a million pieces and fell to the floor. She looked around the room. Rage was building up inside her again. She wondered how many times in one night her adrenaline could soar and drop before she completely went mad. She just wanted to check on her dad and be with Nate before the police showed up and carted them all away.

There was no sign of her dad. She took a couple of steps inside.

Chapter 27

Sarah glanced around the room. It was silent except for the fire crackling and popping softly in the fireplace. She still didn't see her dad anywhere, or the gun she had seen in his hand a short time ago. In her gut, she knew he was here.

She walked over to the chair in front of his desk. Where Nate had been standing. She ran her hand over the fabric on its back and then down the smooth wooden arm. She sat down on the arm for a moment. Memories filled her mind and overflowed through her eyes.

She was a small child, sitting there on the floor between the fireplace and the big wooden desk. She was coloring in coloring books and he got down on the floor with her. He was always so impressed with her scribbles. She recalled how he would pick up a crayon, ask her what color it was and what item on the page should be that color. She would tell him one thing and he would scribble over another. She would look at him and say 'daddy!' and they would laugh.

She stood up off the arm of the chair and tip toed over to the space between the desk and the fireplace. She turned her head to the right and that's where she found him. He looked as though he just crumpled into a heap on the floor.

His knees were bent upward toward his chest. His hands cupped over a dark purple spot on an otherwise light blue shirt. Blood had spread out around the front of him, crawling toward the desk, as if it was trying to get out of the room. Eventually giving up and just soaking into the carpet.

She sobbed and sank down on the floor. Her knees landed right in the cold wetness of the blood-soaked carpet. She leaned over and stroked her dad's hair. She willed him to breathe. To move, to do something. 'Dad.' She whispered. She stared at his crumpled body lying there on the floor and couldn't hold back the tears.

She had no idea why he had even pulled the gun out. She looked around but didn't see it. After a few moments more of sitting and staring at the top of his head, she slid her gaze out the length of his body. She noticed something in his left hand. She scooted across the wet floor and peeled it out of his hand. It was a card from the rolodex and it had Latham's contact information on it.

Suddenly, it clicked in her mind what he was doing. He was going to call Latham over and get him to explain things to him. He was angry, and Nate was just nervous. 'Oh god dad. I'm so sorry.'

She kissed him on the forehead. She had to go. She knew Latham would get impatient and come inside looking for her. She had to get to him first. He wouldn't expect her to be coming fully enraged. She stood up, tucked the card into her pants pocket, and stomped out of the study.

Chapter 28

Sophie looked at her phone. She had called Sarah to see when she was coming back to get her, so they could have one hell of a talk. It rang several times and then went to her voicemail. She dialed Todd. He answered.

'Well hello sweetness. Things going well?'

'Yeah, sure. Could you bring me the handcuff key?'

'Huh?'

'The handcuff key. You know, there in the nightstand on my side of the bed. Could you bring it to me please?'

Confused, and still half asleep, he sat up trying to make sense of what she had just said. 'Wait, where are you and why do you need a handcuff key?'

'I'm in Sarah's basement. She shackled me to a table and went upstairs. I need that key. Just bring it, please!' She sounded pissed, but not panicked. He made a joke.

'So, things did get a little interesting, huh?'

'Sure. Could you just bring me the key please?'

'Alright baby, I'll be right there. How do I get to you?'

'Come around the garage and through the gate. There is a double door leading down into here. Don't forget that key!'

'Ok, just hold on. I'll be right there.'

Sophie hung up and tried Sarah again. Again, she got several rings and then her voicemail. This time, she left a message.

'Hey Sarah, would you get your ass down here and unchain me. Then tell me what the fuck is going on? Or...just call me back and let me know everything is ok?'

She hung up and laid her phone down on the table next to her. She waited several minutes and then Todd came through the double doors that led down a short set of steps into the basement.

He looked around the room. There were old tools, chests, and tables all over the place. He slipped through the maze of junk and stopped a few feet shy of where Sophie was half sitting on the table. A scowl on her face.

'Not what you had in mind, huh?' Todd asked, an eyebrow raised.

'Shut up. Did you bring it?'

Todd reached deep into his jeans pocket and held up a silver key. 'Yeah, I brought it. What are you gonna do for it?' He wiggled his hips. Seeing her, chained to a table, in an unfamiliar place, did something to him. He would make a game out of it.

She glared at him. She wanted to be angry, but really, with him standing there, wiggling his hips at her, indicating he could ravage her right then and there, her nipples peaked. It was kind of a hot idea for her.

'Chained to a table in a strange place. Hmmm, I don't know that I could do anything. What do you have in mind?'

He smirked and then pulled his shirt off over his head. He tossed it to her and it landed right in her lap.

'Laundry? Really?' She winked at him.

He threw his head back and laughed out loud. The guffaw echoed through the seemingly cluttered space. 'No, but I do intend to get dirty.' He drew his brows together and walked the last few steps towards her with confidence.

Sophie squealed with delight as Todd strode toward her. Her mind lost complete control when he looked at her like this. Her body took over and she was helpless to stop it. She had to have him inside her. Her nipples reached out to him. As he got nearer to her, twitches, tingles, and shivers moved her in places she was otherwise unaware she even had.

When he was standing directly in front of her, he dropped his pants. His semi hard length falling gently against her legs. He gently reached down and pulled her legs up around him. He pressed himself firmly against her.

Sophie exhaled a sigh and squeezed her legs tightly around him, rocking her hips slightly, sliding herself up and down his quickly hardening shaft. He leaned forward and put his hands on the table on either side of her and bucked his hips gently into her.

She moaned softly into his ear. Her mouth slightly opened, her breaths becoming harder and shorter with every thrust against her. She laid back on the table and unfastened her pants, her legs still wrapped snugly around him.

A low, guttural, growl rolled out of Todd's mouth. His hands came up and slid under her shirt. She had unintentionally forgotten her bra. He squeezed and palmed her perky breasts and rolled his thumbs over her hard nipples. He leaned over her and kissed her lips. He pressed himself hard against her, and then rocked his hips softly. She groaned under his mouth.

He ran his hands down her stomach and around her back, sliding them into the back of her jeans. He slid them downward toward his hips, as he stood upright; he lifted her, slipped them off of her ass, and had his rock-hard cock resting on top of her soft mound in a single motion. He rocked gently again, sliding it a mere inch in either direction, ever so slowly.

Sophie unwrapped her legs from around him and brought them up over his shoulders. Todd ran his hands up under her ass and down her thighs, He knew she wanted him to rip her jeans right off, but he was going to make her wait. He enjoyed the way his patience tormented her. How when she just couldn't take anymore teasing, her eyes would grow dark and sinister. Like she was about to throw him down and take what she wanted from him.

She didn't have the look yet. He left her jeans around her knees, her back on the table, hand shackled to the table, and exposed to him. He leaned over her and kissed her again. Then he wrapped his arms around her waist and lifted and pulled her down to where just her back was on the table. Her ass was hanging off but supported by his strong thick thighs. His erection slid up over her stomach, nearly reaching her naval, his balls pressed firmly against her ass.

He placed one hand on her breasts and the other he brought around her knees and slid gently down the backs of her thighs and back up again. Goosebumps spread over her skin. She caught her breath and held it, while she bit her lower lip.

This last pass of his hand down the backs of her thighs did not stop at her crease this time. Instead, it slid right in between her thighs and downward. His dick still resting over her mound, he spread her lips from one side and then the other, letting himself slip right between them. He sucked in a breath when her warmth and wetness finally made contact with his skin.

It was this moment that he wondered if he could hold out long enough for her. His body ached to be inside her. He banged his legs with some force against the table, checking it for stability. His eyes met hers and they both nodded.

He brought his other hand down and grabbed himself by the base of the shaft and balls. He tilted his hand upward, lifting his erection off of her. With his other hand, he rubbed and fondled around her softest parts. He found her bump and circled it with his thumb, at the same time he slipped his pinky into her wet spot and moved both of them in a circular motion.

Her head tilted backwards. Her hands clenched his biceps and she pulled him toward her as she rocked against his fingers. 'Oh Jesus Todd. Now!' She was on the verge of climax and he had barely even touched her. She rocked hard into him.

Todd pulled his hips backwards, lowered his erection right directly in line with his pinky, and pressed slowly. She was soaked. He knew he would slip right in, but he chose to take it as slowly as possible, at first.

He replaced his pinky with the tip of his dick. He pushed and pulled a few times. Sophie's hips rocked hard, trying to get a grip on him and pull more of him into her. He wouldn't have it yet. He pulled completely away, just briefly. He pushed the head back in, and a little more, then back out again. A little at a time until his entire length was inside her. He pressed his hips firmly against her ass and held there.

He really enjoyed how her pussy wrapped around him, and then throbbed. He never knew how she was able to do it, but there had been several times that she had him coming and he never had to thrust at all. Just stay there and let her muscles do all the work. That wasn't going to cut it this time though. He needed force.

She was lost, her mind completely blank. Her body doing all the feeling, thinking, or not thinking. Just feeling him all the way inside her took her breath away and made every muscle in her body throb and twitch. She inhaled, trying to get a deep breath, when he bucked against her. A moan came with her exhale.

He rocked on his feet, shifting his weight and pulling out of her almost all the way, and then thrusting his hips forward, rammed himself into her. He repeated the motion slowly at first. He worked up to a nice, constant rhythm. Sophie's breaths were growing shorter and became more like whimpers and her head rolled side to side.

Her nails dug into his arms and her hips tightened against him. He shortened his strokes and picked up the pace. His hips slamming into her ass, making a clicking clapping sound. He kept it up until her breathing was coming in full on moans, her eyes were rolled back in her head, and her insides grew slick and warm around him. He slowed his pace and let her catch her breath. She looked up at him, eyes glossy and full of bliss. He leaned over and kissed her hard on the lips.

He pulled out and backed away from her, dropping her legs to the floor. She stood and looked at him, confused. He put one finger in the air and twirled it. When he saw that she was still confused, he grabbed her by the shoulders and turned her around. Her shackled arm now crossing her body, he bent her forward over the table.

'Oh ho ho, why didn't you say so?' She laid out over the table, presenting her ass to him to do as he pleased.

'Shhh, the only noise I want to hear is you moaning and the table creaking.'

Once she was bent over the table and adjusted her arm so that it wouldn't be breaking in the restraint, tucked up under her breasts. She spread her legs and just leaned on the table. She lifted her head off the table and nodded.

Todd stepped back up against her. He pressed his hips against her ass. His erection was fading slightly, but being pressed against her slit, bent over the table it was back to hard as brick in no time. He took it in his hand again and ran it up and down from just above her asshole to her clit. He repeated the motion until she rocked backward on her heels and pushed herself onto him.

He grunted as her warm wet pussy gripped him and pulled him into her deeper. He smacked her ass. 'That is how it's gonna be then.' He bent over her, shoving her knees against the table. He shoved himself into her, and then slid his feet forward, holding her in place. He put his hands on her lower back and leveraged himself. He thrust into her, harder and harder.

She whimpered at first, but it wasn't long before her whimpers became muffled screams. He grabbed a handful of her hair and pulled her head backwards. He wanted to hear her. The table creaked and squeaked with each thrust, banging into the wooden pillar beside it.

Neither of them paid much attention to it, but the pillar was holding a chain. The chain was attached to a rack hanging above their heads. The dim light of the room failed to shine off the rusted blades and points of the old farm tools dangling above their heads.

Sophie was on the verge of orgasm. He could feel it building. Her body tightened and her vagina squeezed him tighter with each stroke. He dug his fingers into her ass, pulling her to him as he picked up the pace and the intensity. His third thrust at near hyper speed caused a loud crack. Now he was on the verge also.

As Sophie's climax took over her, tools came crashing down around her. A pickaxe crashed onto the table beside her and fell on its side. A shovel handle landed sideways across the middle of her back. Then so did Todd.

Chapter 29

She never felt him come. Just go stiff, then limp, and then he fell over on top of her. She laughed. Feeling lucky that the blades and things had missed them, she tried to turn over. She was stuck. 'Todd, sweetie, let me up now.' She turned and looked behind her and his eyes were wide, blankly staring at her. Blood was dripping down his forehead and onto her back. A scythe blade was buried in his skull and was sticking out of the top of his head.

She struggled to get out from under him. He was heavy on top of her and her hand was still shackled to the table. 'The key. Todd, where is the key?' She half expected him to answer her.

She had watched him pull it out of his front right pocket of his jeans that were now lying on the floor behind her. 'Fuck.' She laid her head down on the table. She couldn't panic. The thought was crossing her mind now. Sarah would be coming back down and she did not want her to catch them like this. 'Avoid thinking about Todd's current condition. Just breathe. Think.'

She had no idea what other tools had fallen onto him, what was still hanging above her, and what else could fall and end her the same way as him. Not the way she wanted to go. She looked around, moving as little as possible. She reached back and felt around gently, barely touching Todd and cringing. 'Don't think about it right now. Just get the fuck out of here.'

She slid her body backwards toward Todd, pushing her body against his, gently and slowly, until he fell backwards and off of her. He slumped to the floor and landed with a clang of metal. She stood up and assessed the situation around her. Her pants still around her knees, she pulled them up and fastened them. Then she looked around on the floor for Todd's jeans.

She spotted them lying just a few feet away. Not close enough to reach with her hands, but she slid her foot over and was still shy of reaching them by a few inches. Not enough to even grab with her toes and pull to her. She leaned back against the table and cursed. 'Fuck.'

She stood there for a long while, looking over the mess of tools sprawled all around her. She rolled her eyes. She reached over and picked up the shovel that had fallen to the floor right beside the table when she slid out from under Todd. She stepped as far away from the table as she could. She gained the few inches that she was lacking with the shovel. She pulled the jeans close enough to her to grab them and dropped the shovel. She dug into each pocket until she found the one with the key in it. She pulled the key out and kissed it and then shoved it in the lock.

She turned the key and the cuff fell loose. She rubbed her wrist and looked around again. Todd now laid crumpled and naked on the floor in front other. While she didn't consider him the love of her life. She cared very deeply for him. Seeing him lying there like that broke her. She ran over to him and held him for a moment. 'Oh Todd, baby, I'm soooo sorry.' She lifted his hand to her face and rubbed her cheek with it, then showered it with kisses.

She heard what she thought was stomping through the kitchen upstairs and then heard the back door open and close. She sat with Todd for a while. Crying, kissing his hand, and apologizing.

She pulled herself together and stood up. She looked down at herself, covered in Todd's blood, front and back. She knew she should call the police, but she needed to find out what was going on with Sarah first.

She stomped up the basement steps and walked into the kitchen. It was just as it was before she and Sarah went down to the basement, except for the puddle of blood and the body on the floor. She avoided stepping in it and went around the other side of the island, careful not to touch anything.

She ran up the stairs, toward Sarah's room. She found Nate's body lying on the floor in the hallway, a blood-soaked umbrella lying right next to him. She gasped. This was not good. Not good at all. 'Awww, Nate.' She avoided touching him too. When she stood up, she realized she had stepped into the blood that had soaked into the carpet there. She slipped her shoes off, backed away, careful not to step in anymore blood, turned and ran back down stairs.

She stopped at the open door of the study. It was wide open and the light was on. She stepped into the well-lit room. If she was next, she wanted to be in a bright place. She looked around. She didn't see anyone there either though. She pulled her phone out of her pocket and dialed Sarah's number. Straight to voicemail. She gazed around the room and spotted a cell phone broken to pieces lying near the opposite wall. She walked over to it and picked several of the pieces up. It was Sarah's. That's when she saw him out of the corner of her eye.

Jacob was lying on the floor, looking at her from under his desk. His lifeless eyes just staring at her. She walked over and around the desk. A gun laid just a foot from where he had fallen. She knelt down at his feet and looked him over. One side of his shirt was blood soaked, darker near the middle of his chest, almost hiding the small hole that was now present. The carpet beneath him was a shiny crimson, a little behind him, but a lot in front of him, seeming to creep toward the door.

Another one dead. 'Jesus, let me find Sarah alive so I don't have to hunt down and kill that Latham guy.' She whispered to herself. She stood there for a minute, looking back and forth between the gun and Jacob. Her thoughts raced. 'What the fuck is going on here?'

She tried to piece together what had happened here. Jacob was shot in the chest, Nate was stabbed in the gut with an umbrella, and Olivia was beaten to death. Where was Sarah? The guest house entered her thoughts. She shook her head. She didn't want to go back into that place ever again. Or the basement, for that matter. She had to find Sarah though. She picked up the gun.

She held it in one hand and tip toed all the way to the back door.

Chapter 30

Sarah stormed out of the study, through the entry way at the bottom of the stairs, and through the kitchen. She didn't pause for a moment to look at the mess that was her mom on her way to the back door. She did spare a glance toward the basement door way but decided that was the safest place for Sophie at the moment.

She burst through the back door and trod heavily all the way to the guest house. Latham was there, in the chair, waiting for her. 'What the hell...What the hell happened to you?'

'I told you it wasn't a good time. You had to insist though, so here I am. Dad is dead, mom is dead, Nate is dead. So go ahead and push me. You can end up like them too. You deserve it for all the shit you have done! What the fuck do you want?'

Latham stood up. Even seeing her covered in blood, he denied believing that she had killed anyone. Not Sarah.

She saw him stand up and step toward her. She glanced around the room for the object nearest to her. The fireplace poker, solid silver and long with a pointed tip, was immediately to her left. She side stepped and pulled it off the holder.

Latham paused just in front of where she had been standing. 'What the hell do you think you are doing?' Put that down and come talk to me. We have a problem.' He put his hands up like she was pointing a gun at him.

'Take one more step toward me and I'll show you' She slung the poker up over her shoulder like it was a bat.

'Sarah. Stop this. You know you won't swing that at me. Not and live to tell about it.' His eyes grew narrow and a grin spread across his face. He took a step toward her and she swung. She caught him in the shoulder with the hook. She was not kidding.

'God Dammit! What the hell is your problem tonight? I called you out here so we could talk about our problem and not get attacked by that flea bitten beast you call a cat again. Give me that!' He reached, with his good arm for the poker. She pulled it back and swung it again. She nailed him in the elbow with the bar. He bellowed and pulled his arm back.

'I've got no problem. You have the problem. You will turn around and leave here the way you came or you will leave in a body bag with everyone else. The choice is yours. I'm not fucking around Latham. Get the hell out!' She didn't want to kill him. She hated him and wanted him to die, but she had enough blood on her hands. She gave him one chance.

With both if his arms screaming at him painfully, there wasn't much he could do. 'Yeah right. I can't even drive now bitch. You are stuck with me...' He took a step backwards and turned toward the chair he had been seated in. 'Come bandage this shit or something.'

'Fuck you!' She brought the poker up again, ready to swing. She had warned him.

He turned back toward her and took one long stride. He grabbed her by her throat. He walked backward and dragged her with him to the chair. Her arms dropped to her sides as she struggled to keep her balance. She brought the one with the poker in it back up and placed the sharp point just under his chin.

He released her as he raised his hands in a defensive manner and sat down in the chair. She moved forward jabbed the point into his neck. Certain it has pierced his skin; she applied just enough pressure to keep him in a submissive position. 'I warned you. You should have listened.' She gave a quick jab and watched almost gleefully as a large drop of red liquid slid down the side of the silver rod.

'Ok. Stop. I'll leave you alone. Just, dammit, I'm bleeding all over the place here. Help me stop the bleeding.' He'd learned recently that the sight of his own blood had a tendency to make him queasy and weak. The last thing he wanted to do right this moment was appear weak. He spoke firmly. 'We have to discuss this problem.'

'What is this problem you seem to think we have Latham?' The only problem I can see that WE have is you not taking me seriously when I told you to get the hell out.'

'You know. That guy your dad killed?' Latham shot an eyebrow up at her. Expecting that it would distract her. 'He's not dead. He's at my house. Alive and well. Well sort of.'

She didn't react at all. She answered simply. 'He's your problem. Not mine.'

'That's not exactly true now, and you know it. He's your real father. You're going to turn your back on him?'

The hottest fire roared through her veins. She had been shutting that information out all this time. Her real father was dead on the floor in the study. Always would be. She didn't care what this stranger, or anyone else said. Jacob Rosenthal was her father. 'What does that have to do with anything?'

Latham was taken back. He didn't take Sarah for the uncaring type. 'Just that he's sick and I don't know what to do about it. You really don't care?'

'You bastard!' She spit the words out at him.

'Watch your mouth. I'm only winged here. We are talking. No violence.' He had to get her guard down and he wasn't sure what more he could do. He wasn't sure what he was going to do when it was, but she was going to pay for all of this.

She stared into his eyes. Pressing the poker firmly into his neck. She was in control now. She knew it when she watched his eyes go wide and his head lean back as far as it could against the chair. She decided to toy with him a bit. 'Ok, so talk. Apologize for all the shit you have done to me over the past week. And do it like you mean it.'

He sat up straight. He would not apologize for anything. She may have him at a disadvantage at the moment but he would never apologize. He did what he had to do to keep her quiet. If she told anyone about what had happened, it would be the end of the money from Jacob and he couldn't afford that.

'No. I'm not going to apologize. You think because you have a stick and have made me bleed that I'm going to say that I felt the least bit bad about what I've done to you? You are sadly mistaken.' He stood up, the point of the poker digging deeper into his throat. He pressed the issue. 'I'll do it again. When I'm done with you, I'll go after your little bitch friend again too.'

Her blood ran cold. The fire that had been burning in her veins just a few moments before had frozen instantly. The realization that he had actually raped Sophie was more than she could handle. She pulled her arm back and went to shove it into him as hard as she could. She watched him swallow and aimed her blow to that exact spot. It wasn't a necessarily sharp object, but she was confident, as angry as she was, that she had the force to end him.

She pushed forward and up as hard as she could. Blood dripped from the end of the poker. She smiled. His hands came up and grabbed the poker and shoved it back toward her with both hands. The force of his shove made her lose her grip on the handle and threw her backward, She fell to the floor on her butt about two feet away. The poker dropped to the floor with a dull clang. It landed directly between him and her. She scooted forward to grab it but he made it to it first.

She scanned the immediate area. The only thing within her reach was the cord to the lamp sitting on the table beside the chair. She grabbed it and yanked. The lamp wobbled, swirling the light in the room just long enough to distract him for a split second.

She kicked him square in the knee with all her might and he stumbled a little. He bent forward and grabbed his knee with one hand and cussed. She stood up, grabbed the lamp and smashed it into his head. The ceramic base shattered to pieces all over the floor. Blood dripped from her hand and the side of his head, but he did not fall. He swirled slightly on his feet.

He steadied himself. 'Is that all you got bitch?' Come on. It's a fight now.' He reared back and swung the poker up over his head. A loud bang filled the room.

Chapter 31

Sophie tip toed through the hall between the study and the kitchen. She looked up to the top of the stairs. Knowing Nate was up there, she said a quiet prayer and promised him that she would be back, with Sarah, and they would take care of him.

She stalled for a long moment, recalling hearing the back-door latch as she was coming up the basement stairs. She hadn't heard any kind of struggle or screams, but she hadn't heard a gunshot either. She realized that was probably why Sarah trapped her in the basement. 'Oh God Sarah, what the hell happened here?'

Never in a million years would she think, even for a second, that this massacre could have been done by Sarah. Her only thought and fear was that Latham had done this, and now he had Sarah in the guest house. She continued walking confidently toward the back door. The gun drawn and held like a cop clearing a crime scene. He would not be hurting her friend again.

She peeked her head around the fridge in the kitchen, making sure no one was standing on the other side of it. She didn't know if she could handle any surprises. There was no one there. Olivia was still on the floor in a bloody puddle between her and the back door. She stepped to the opposite side of the island, between it and the dining room table.

She reached the back door and thought she heard something behind her. She spun around, gun pointing, waiting for someone to jump out at her. She held her breath, listening. Her heart was racing, she inhaled, trying to calm herself. When she didn't hear anything but the refrigerator running, she turned back to the door and exhaled.

She opened the door slowly. She remembered the night before in the guest house. She had managed to escape, sort of unscathed, but the fact that he had shown up with the intention of raping her made her skin crawl. She had prepared for the worst-case scenario, but she didn't really expect him to show back up. It was literally the only thing that saved her. She shook with the realization.

She stood at the door. Hesitant to go any further. Her gut twisted and turned as she pleaded with herself to continue. Fear was freezing her in place. She reminded herself that it was just a place, and Sarah was there.

The thought of Sarah being raped by that monster again and possibly killed this time flashed through her mind. She saw something move in the doorway of the guest house across the yard. It wasn't a huge yard, but it was far enough across it that she had a hard time making out what was going on. She watched for a moment before she realized it was Sarah. She saw her fly backward and land hard on her ass.

Sophie took off like a bullet, running toward the guest house. She arrived just as Latham was about to bring a fireplace poker down over his head and into Sarah's. She raised the gun to eye level with both hands and pulled the trigger. She fired one shot. She watched as Latham jerked backward from the impact and fell into the chair behind him in slow motion.

～

SOPHIE STOOD THERE, waiting for him to get up. When he didn't so much as take a breath after a long moment, she looked around the room. Then at Sarah. She was covered in blood. Her hand was dripping large drops of crimson onto the floor. She was shaking.

Sarah, filled with rage again, took advantage of the situation. She picked up the broken lamp again and beat Latham about his head and chest. She didn't notice Sophie standing in the doorway, gun still aimed and smoking.

Sophie stepped into the room and waited for the beating to stop. She could only imagine the amount of rage and hatred she had for the man. She knew she would stop eventually, so she waited patiently for her to stop.

Sarah pummeled and beat Latham's dead body until the copper tubing bent and was useless. She dropped it and picked up the poker. She continued to beat him, with water-soaked eyes and snot bubbling from her nose. She kept swinging until she could no longer breathe. When she finally stopped, she stepped backward, drops the poker and gasped for air.

Sophie reached toward Sarah and called her name. 'Sarah.' Sarah jumped three feet in the air when she felt a hand on her shoulder.

Sarah balled up her fists and turned toward the voice. Sophie backed away a step and put her hands up. 'It's me. Sophie. Soph. Are you ok sweetie?' Her voice as soft and soothing as she could make it.

Sarah's hands came down and she flew into Sophie's chest. Her head landed on her should and she sobbed uncontrollably. Sophie wrapped her arms around her and they both fell to the floor. She held Sarah as tight as she could until she could talk again.

Sarah pulled away from Sophie. She turned around and stared at Latham's body, still sitting there in the chair. She had made a real mess. She turned around and sat facing him. She tilted her head to the right and then to the left. She exhaled slowly.

Sophie scooted up next to her. She watched Sarah start at Latham for a moment and saw a sense of calm take over her. She looked back and forth between the two of them. The look on Sarah's face was strange. It was a simple grin, but instead of looking happy, she looked, dazed. 'Are you alright?'

Sarah wouldn't take her eyes off of Latham. She heard Sophie's question and contemplated it before she responded. 'Am I alright? As long as he doesn't get back up, I will be.' She continued to watch him for moment longer. When his chest didn't rise and fall as it should if he was breathing, she looked at Sophie. 'Yep. I'm fine. The look on her face didn't change.

Sophie inhaled deeply and exhaled. She wasn't sure what to say. The vibe in the room was surreal and strange. She was happy that Latham was dead, but she was sitting here, covered in Todd's blood, watching Sarah stare. She spoke quietly. 'That bad?'

'Yep.'

'Why didn't you tell me?'

Sarah thought for a long moment. She looked at Latham again. Tilting her head from side to side as if she was looking at an abstract painting in an art gallery. 'Because then we wouldn't have this beautiful work of art you see here now.'

Sophie laughed out loud. She couldn't have helped it if she wanted too. She put her arm around Sarah's shoulder. 'Oh. Right.' They both sat and stared at him for a while.

Chapter 32

After a few moments of staring, Sarah turned to Sophie. 'How did you get out of the basement?'

'Todd.' Sophie almost whispered his name. She looked down at the floor. The memory of him lying there on the floor, naked, with a scythe sticking out of the top of his head brought tears to her eyes.

'Where is he at now?'

'Basement.'

Sarah turned and looked at Sophie. 'Why?'

'Dead.'

'What? How?'

It was Sophie's turn to hesitate an answer. The events that led up to his death flooded her brain, and guilt washed over her. 'Scythe."

Sophie and Sarah both knew that they would need to call the police. Explain the situation to them. Sarah knew she would be going away for a very long, long time. With the death of Nate and her mom, and now Latham on her hands. The thoughts pounded through her brain and made her feel ill. She turned and looked at Sophie.

'Oh God Soph, what have I done?' Sarah's eyes repeated the question.

Sophie thought for a very long time. 'What do you mean what have you done? You haven't done anything."

'Soph, I...'

'You fought for your life. He was a monster, and he needed to die. I am the one that killed him anyway. You have nothing to worry about.'

'But...what about...Nate...' Tears filled her eyes. 'And...my dad...my mom?"

'We will deal with that. Tell me what happened.'

'I don't know, really. It's mostly a blur. There was just chaos. Too much to deal with inside my head. Nate showed up, he was in with my dad. I peeked. I should never peek.' She buried her head in her hands and sobbed.

Sophie placed her hand on Sarah's back and rubbed in a circle gently. 'We will figure all that out. Take a breath." She waited for Sarah to pull herself together.

Sarah inhaled a stuttered breath, held it for a moment, and exhaled. Repeated. When the boulder in the pit of her stomach was the size of a pea again, she spoke. 'I killed him Soph. I loved him, but I killed him."

'What are you talking about? Latham killed him. He killed all of them, well except for Todd. And he was about to kill you. We had no choice but to kill him.'

'What? No Soph, that's not what happened.'

'Sure it is. It has to be.'

'Soph...' Sophie cut her off.

'Sarah, it is what happened. Nate came and talked to your father. Latham showed up.' Sophie saw it all in her head. She needed to make Sarah see it, even if she knew better.

'What?'

'Sarah, if you tell them that you did any of it, you will be responsible for all of it. You couldn't hurt anyone, Latham could. Did. He needed to be stopped. He caught you in the guest house, started beating you, and when I came and saw it, I shot him.'

'Sophie. I can't do that. It's not the truth. I am responsible, for all of it.'

Sophie shook her head. Both to indicate her disagreement, and to shake the thought that Sarah was capable of the massacre from her mind. 'Sarah, do you want to go to prison?'

'No. but...'

'Just answer the questions I ask. Would you ever hurt anyone else?'

'No.'

'With the exception of Nate, did they deserve it?'

Sarah thought about Nate. His body lying in a puddle upstairs. His glassy lifeless eyes. His last words to her. Her eyes filled with water and spilled over. She shook her head and thought about her mom. How cruel she had been with her words.

'I didn't kill my dad. He dropped the gun and it went off.'

'No Sarah. Get it straight. Latham killed everyone.' She took Sarah's face in her hands. 'You have to get it straight. You don't deserve to spend the rest of your life in prison for this. None of them are worth that. Sarah, are you hearing me?'

'Sophie...I don't know if I can...'

'You have to. If you don't, we will both get blamed for all of it. Latham is dead. You don't have to be afraid anymore. Just think about it for a minute.'

Sarah thought, but the only thing going through her mind was Nate. His last words rolled through her brain, on loop. None of that mattered now. Nate, the only person she wanted to spend the rest of her life with, was gone. It didn't matter if she went to prison or not. Her knowing that she killed him would punish her for the rest of her life.

'No Soph. I have to tell the truth. I can't live with anymore secrets.'

'Sarah...'

'Sophie, listen to me. A few days ago, I watched my dad kill a man. Shortly after that, Latham became my stalker. I'm pretty sure he was around to keep me quiet. He, for some reason, got the idea that if he scared me to death for my life and the life of everyone I cared about, he could keep me quiet. It worked. That's over now. It can all come out, and it won't hurt my dad anymore, won't hurt me anymore. I'm not going to lie, and start a whole new life with another secret. I'll do my time, and maybe, after, I'll be able to live a normal life.'

'Sarah...' Sophie thought about how terrible life was going to be for Sarah now. She didn't deserve what was going to happen to her next though. 'We have to tell them something else. You don't deserve that.'

'It won't work any other way. I killed Nate, and my mom. Nate was an accident. My mom...I don't know what that was. Latham was not abusing me when you found me. I had turned on him.'

'He was about to pound you in the head with a fireplace poker!'

'It was self defense. I had already stabbed him several times and I was about to rip his jugular out with it, until he grabbed it and shoved me away. I kinda wish he had killed me. Then it would all truly be over.'

'Don't talk like that. He raped you. Just once and he deserved to die. You know he would have again, if I hadn't showed up.'

Sarah turns and looks at Sophie. Tears rolled down her cheeks. 'And you. He raped you too. Oh god. I'm so sorry Soph.'

'No sweetie. He did not. He tried to. I stabbed him with my little pig sticker and he ran out crying like a baby. So stop it! No one deserves what he did to you, what he tried to do to me. Or what he was trying to do to your dad. Whatever that was. He needed to die, so you and I could live without any more fear.'

'How will you live without fear now? Wondering constantly if someone will figure out what actually happened.'

'We figure that out when it comes up. We live, fear free, in the meantime. Don't do this Sarah. I'll help you through it, just don't give up.'

'I can't Sophie. I just can't.'

Chapter 33

DJ parks his big brown truck across the street from the Rosenthal residence. He picks up his scanner and heads to the back. It is early evening, and it is his second to last stop for the day.

It was an uneventful day up until his lunch break. His supervisor called him and asked him to meet up with another driver and take the remainder of his deliveries. It was only a few pieces, but it was enough to put him way behind schedule on his own route.

He was normally done with his route two hours earlier. The Rosenthal's was the most out of the way; he enjoyed making them the last stop. He liked them. They were friendly, and he had been delivering to them for many years now. They often conversed with him, keeping him there longer than he stayed at any of his regular stops. He enjoyed the conversation though, so he didn't mind it. Especially with Sarah.

Tonight though, behind schedule and tired, he would try to keep the conversation short. He picked up and scanned five packages and set them by the back against the roll up door. Checking his scanner to confirm again that he had gathered all of their packages, he nodded, hung his scanner on a clip on his belt and headed to the door.

He looked at the house across the street. He could see into the large window to the right of the front door. It was Mr. Rosenthal's office. He would often see him sitting at his desk. Mr. Rosenthal would usually be the one to open the door. He assumed tonight would be no different. He picked up the packages, stacking them on top of each other in one arm. The final one he carried in his free hand. He headed across the street.

As he neared the front door, he noticed that Mr. Rosenthal was standing behind his desk. He didn't think anything of it until he stepped on to the porch and heard a loud bang. He tilted his head toward the sound. He took the two remaining steps to the front door and reached for the doorbell. He looked through the glass on the front door and saw someone running up the stairs inside.

He dropped the packages on the porch and darted back to his truck. He picked up his cell phone and dialed 911. The phone beeped in his ear. 'Dammit. No signal.' He sat there in his truck, contemplating what his next step should be. If he left the scene, made the call, they might figure him the prime suspect, even if he came back. He needed to find out more about what had happened. He heard a gunshot, but at that moment, had no idea if anyone had been hit.

The fact that it was the senator's house made it something that needed to be kept quiet until all the details were known. DJ liked this family. There was no reason to speculate, call in a bunch of speculators, and have a scandal over nothing. He was well known enough with them that it wouldn't be seen as breaking and entering if he was to take a look around. If he found anything afoul, he could use the phone inside to call for help.

'Better idea than running from the scene'. He told himself. He got out of his truck, his phone still in one hand keys with dog repellent attached, in the other, and headed back to the house. When he reached the porch, he stepped to the left and looked in the window. He didn't see anyone in the room now. He stepped back over to the front door, checked the handle. It was unlocked. He stepped inside.

From his position in the front hall, he could see in either direction, from the outside wall in the living room to the back door of the kitchen. He took a few steps to the left and peeked into the study. He looked around the room. He saw pieces of a cell phone lying on the floor across the room. He took the few steps toward the broken cell phone. He leaned over to pick up a piece and out of the corner of his eye, he saw him.

The senator, lying on the floor, staring blankly at him. He jumped up, ran to the edge of the desk. There he saw the body curled up on the floor. He crouched; leaned in to touch the senator, checking for signs of life he knew he wouldn't find when he heard what he thought was the backdoor slamming shut.

DJ stood up quickly, almost making himself dizzy. He turned, grabbed the dog repellent hanging out of his pocket, and held it up in front of him. He crept to the doorway and peeked around the corner. Shielding himself from view of anyone that might be in the house with him, although assuming that whoever slammed the back door had gone out, not come in.

He didn't see anyone moving around in the kitchen. He crouched down and listened at the door way for a solid minute. He didn't hear any movement, just the hum of the refrigerator. The furnace kicked on suddenly, startling him, until the chill of the room was pushed out past him through the doorway and he realized what the new sound was. He calmed himself with a few deep breaths and stepped out of the room back in the front hall.

His dog repellent in his hand and held up in front of him he slipped through the hallway toward the kitchen. How he wished he had a gun right now. The thought crossed his mind, what kind of damage was he going to do with pepper spray against a full-grown man? He shrugged it off. He was far too hyped, right now, to have a gun. He reasoned it out.

If Sarah or Mrs. Rosenthal stepped out from around a corner, he would probably pull the trigger before he even realized it. At least right now, if that happened, she would just get burning eyes. If it was the gunman, he would at least be temporarily blinded and he could grab and restrain him.

He peered up the stairs. He had seen someone run up the stairs immediately after the gun shot. He considered going up, but he had heard the back door slam. He stuck with his assumption that if the gunman was up there, he was better off down here. He could sneak up on him if he was outside or catch him jumping the fence or something. If he was upstairs, he could ambush him while he was stumbling around in the dark, waiting for his eyes to adjust. He continued on to the kitchen.

As soon as he stepped into the kitchen, he wanted to be sick. The slightly metallic smell of drying blood and bodily fluids stung his nose. The small hallway had given a straight view of the back door, over an island, but obscured the view of Mrs. Rosenthal lying on the floor between the sink and the island until he reached the edge of the tile floor.

There was no doubt she was no longer among the living. He didn't bother going over to examine her. The cause of death was almost obvious. Blood, pieces of her skull, and gray matter collected and thickened under her head that had been smashed flat to her ears. Whoever did this was extremely upset, and strong. He shook the image off and proceeded to the back door.

Something low on his right moved, catching his eye. He spun around on one foot and aimed his dog repellent. A large black cat jumped from the window and scurried across the room, slipping and sliding on the slick tile floor, and bolted up the stairs.

When he could breathe again, he turned back toward the back door and noticed the basement stairs to his left, barely lit up from the kitchen and the basement lights. He descended the stairs. In the far corner, he spied an old wooden table, an old rusted rack hanging on one side by a chain and old farm tools scattered around. At the end of the table was a man, shirtless, with a scythe sticking out of the top of his head. Obvious his cause of death. There was a puddle of blood on top of the table and on the floor beneath him.

The scene confused him. As he tried to piece the scene together, he heard another gun shot. It had come from outside the house. It rattled the windows in the basement. It was so loud and close by that he ducked and his hands flew up over his head. He was surprised that he wasn't completely sprawled out on the floor. He waited for a few moments, listening to the sounds, and then stood up. He brushed himself off and headed back up the stairs.

Once back in the kitchen, he looked back down the hallway toward the front door, shielding himself from view until he was certain the coast was clear. He stepped onto the tile and turned to go out the back door.

He opened the door slowly, expecting a loud creak might give him away. He was surprised that it made no sound at all. He stepped out the door into the dark. Standing there on the small concrete slab that served as a step into the house, he looked out across the yard and found the small bungalow type guest house.

The front door was wide open, and it looked like someone was laid back in the chair that faced the door. He opted to remain in the shadows and get a closer look at the person in the chair. As he drew closer, he saw blood. A lot of blood. Splattered on the wall behind the chair and all down the front of the man sitting in the chair. He shook his head.

He watched a hand, low and to the right, and a short distance from the door way. It was waving around, like a person does when they are talking to someone. He took a step to the left and crouched. He wanted a better look at whose hand it was, even though he was pretty certain it was Sarah's.

It was. She was sitting there, on the floor, next to a small dark-haired woman he had never seen before. Both of them were covered in blood. He stood up and headed to the door. He called out. 'Sarah? Sarah, its DJ, the delivery guy. Are you alright?'

Chapter 34

Sarah froze when she heard her name. She stared, wide eyed at Latham sitting there, eyes open looking at a space between the wall and the ceiling. She heard it again. Closer this time. 'Sarah, its Derrick...'

'FUCK!!! What is he doing here?' She jumped to her feet. She was about to yell back to him but he was peeking around the door way, his back against the wall, before she could utter a word. She nodded at him.

He rushed to her and caught her before her knees buckled. The adrenaline that had seethed through her just a short time ago was now completely gone and combined with the head rush of standing up so quickly made her dizzy. She had enough time to process what has happened, but the sound of someone's voice coming from outside, calling her name spiked a rush and left her as quickly as it had peaked. Her body just didn't have the energy to keep her on her feet.

'Are you alright? He spoke into her ear while looking at the other woman in the room, rising to her feet. 'What the hell happened here?'

Sarah opened her mouth to speak. The words jumbled and mashed together. 'Ohmyg...it'suchamess......'

Sophie cut her off. She was shaking but had set the gun down on the floor beside where she had been sitting. She had kept it fixed, reflexively, on Latham while she and Sarah talked, but when a stranger to her showed up she set felt safe enough to set it down.

'He was about to kill her...so I shot him.' She looked over at Latham's body and cringed.

Sarah found the mental acuity to put together a sentence that made sense and enough strength to stand on her own again. The words rushed out. 'We fought and I stabbed him a couple times but he got the poker from me." She took a deep breath to continue. 'What are you doing here?'

DJ rubbed her back. 'Ok. Calm down. I was running behind, helped another driver out. Got to the front porch and heard the gunshot, then saw someone run upstairs. What happened inside?'

Sarah looked at Sophie. She wanted to tell him the truth. Sophie wanted her not to. She didn't want to go prison, but she didn't want to live with another secret. She remained silent.

Sophie saw Sarah look at her, and now both of their eyes were locked on her. She had come up with a scenario of what she imagined had happened as she walked through the house. She hoped that this guy had not gone down into the basement, so left out the part about him.

'I don't know for sure, but it seems like Latham showed up to get another piece of Sarah. Everyone was here and up though. That drove him crazy maybe, so he killed them all until he was able to get to Sarah? I've met the guy and he wasn't real stable, and totally capable. He raped Sarah once and probably would have done it again if I hadn't shot him.' She looked back at Sarah.

'Jesus this was a mess. Why would Sophie say that. She knew that she had killed Nate, and her mom. Her dad was self-inflicted. She was making this up. As good as it sounded, it wasn't the truth. She couldn't stand that.

'No, he didn't.' She was adamant about not having any more secrets. She couldn't, wouldn't lie about it. Even if it meant she went to prison. 'No more secrets Soph.'

DJ looked at her, a puzzled look on his face, and then turned his gaze to Sophie, then back to Sarah. He had no idea what all had taken place, but he was pretty certain that Sarah had not done it. 'Secrets?'

'No. No secrets. I can't handle it anymore.' She shook out of DJ's grasp and stomped across the room to the kitchen.

'Sarah, just tell me what happened. We will work this out.'

'I killed them DJ. Nate and my mom. My dad was an accident.'

DJ couldn't believe his ears. Even hearing her say it, he couldn't believe it. Wouldn't believe it. 'No you didn't Sarah. This guy, this arrogant, ego driven, asshole did it. All of it. I saw it.'

Sarah turned around and looked at him. Her eyes bugging out of her head. 'What???'

'I don't know the motive, but what she came up with seems pretty likely.' He pointed at Sophie.

Sophie nodded.

Sarah slammed her cup down on the counter. If it had been glass instead of plastic it would have shattered in a million pieces. Instead, it bounced and toppled into the sink. 'No. There is no way to pin all of it on him. I'm covered in all of their blood, my fingerprints are on the umbrella and all over my mom. No one will believe it was him. He hadn't even been here.'

Sophie strode across the room. She put an arm around Sarah. 'Listen. It's not your fault, and there is an easy explanation for all of it. Take a breath and think about it.'

Sarah looked at Sophie directly in the eyes. 'You really don't understand. This all happened because of a secret. They are all dead now. Except for me. I don't want that one to die with them, and create more that we have to live with.' She ran her hand through her hair. It was sticky and stiff.

'What secrets Sarah?' DJ probed. 'I've known your family for a very long time now. What kinds of secrets could you possibly have?'

'Oh god. I guess it's all gonna come out now. My dad killed a guy a few days ago, and I saw it. Apparently, he was my real dad. Anyway, Latham was there and cleaned up the mess. He found me in the hall in shock and dragged me out here and raped me.

I guess he thought I would be scared enough to not say anything about it after that. Then he showed up at Bull Shots Monday night. Sophie ran him off, but he caught up with me later. I don't know why he did it that time, or yesterday, but he did. He came here tonight to tell me about a problem of some kind. Something about the guy or something. I don't know. I wasn't really listening to him.'

'Oh god how did I not know all of this? I'm so sorry sweetie. I don't blame you for not wanting anymore secrets, but the alternative is prison, and you've lived through enough hell.' Sophie rubbed her hair.

'Then it seems to me that all of this is his fault, even if it wasn't at his hand. He is indirectly responsible for all of it. Now, he's dead, can't argue the point, and so let him take it all. He deserves that and worse, if you ask me.' DJ looked to Sophie for agreement.

Sophie nodded. 'He's right Sarah. This is all his fault. If we can get that across, then it won't be your fault, no secrets. He has gotten what he deserved. You don't deserve to take the blame for what he did. It's not a secret. The man drove you to it. Don't go down for that.'

Sarah needed to think that over. He had, although indirectly tonight, caused all of it. He had made something sad and horrific even more miserable. She had spent all this time thinking that he was trying to protect her father just as much as she was willing to. Even if it was at her expense. She took a deep breath.

They all three turned their heads toward the front door when they heard sirens coming in the distance.

Chapter 35

When the police arrived, all three of them were standing on the front porch. DJ, having a link to law enforcement through family, had a good idea of what to expect, and he had not had any involvement, so he had no reason to be nervous.

The girls were trembling. Derrick had gone into the living room and looked around for some blankets or coats, anything that would help the girls keep warm. He found a small pile of throw blankets in an old rocking chair in the living room. He grabbed the entire stack and headed back out the door. He handed a couple to Sophie and unfolded one and wrapped it around Sarah, then a second one. He led Sarah over to the steps and helped her sit down. Sophie followed, took a seat next to Sarah, and put her arms around her.

The first squad car pulled up in front of the house. None of the three of them knew who called them and they doubted they would ever find out. It didn't matter, they were here now. Probably a good thing since their stories had to line up, and match the times of death.

The officer remained in his car until a second unit arrived. It pulled up in the street alongside the first. The sirens stopped, but the lights continued to flash. The two officers approached the porch, hands on their guns. Long, bright flashlights scanned back and forth across the yard and then over the house. Their lights crossed and shined directly in their faces as the officers stepped up to the porch.

'Where is the gunman?' The first officer asked.

DJ spoke. 'Guest house, dead. There are three bodies inside, and the one in the guest house.'

'And you are?' The second asked, taking a notepad and pen out of his shirt pocket.

'I'm DJ Roberts.' He pulled out his wallet and handed his driver's license to the officer. 'I drive the big brown truck parked across the street.'

'And you?' He pointed at Sophie.

'Sophie Dunover. I'm her best friend.'

He looked at Sarah, saw the anguish in her face and asked Sophie. 'Her name?'

Sarah whispered, 'Sarah Rosenthal, daughter of the late Jacob and Olivia Rosenthal.'

'What was that?'

Sophie spoke for her. 'Her name is Sarah Rosenthal. As in Senator Jacob Rosenthal's daughter. She is pretty shaken up."

'I can see that. So what happened here?'

The first officer interrupted, 'Do I have permission to go in and take a look around?'

Sarah nodded her head.

'Is there anyone in the house, any weapons I need to be aware of?'

Sophie spoke. 'The only people in the house are dead now, Mr. R is in the study, Mrs. R is in the kitchen, and Nate is upstairs. Todd is in the basement. There is a gun in the guest house on the floor, but the guy in there, Latham I don't know his last name, is dead too.'

Sarah shook. 'Todd, He's really dead too?' She dropped her head into her hands and sobbed.

The first officer cautiously stepped into the house. He stepped to the left, hand on his gun, calling out to anyone that might be there. He stepped to the left and disappeared.

The second officer continued to ask questions. 'We got a call about shots fired at the Senator's house. One at a time, tell me what happened here." He pointed at DJ. 'Let's start with you.'

'I was delivering those packages sitting right over there. I heard a gunshot as soon as I hit the porch, then I saw a big guy run up the stairs. I went back to my truck to call 911 but my phone had no reception. I came back to the house, knocked on the door and tried the handle. I've known the family for a very long time, so I went in to see if there was a problem, and call 911 from if there was.'

'So, were you the one that called?'

'No sir, I don't know who called. I found Mr. Rosenthal on the floor in his study, dead, and I heard the back door slam. I went through the kitchen and found Mrs. Rosenthal on the floor, and then went out the back door, found the girls, and Latham dead in the chair.'

'Alright, then what?'

'We heard the sirens, so I escorted the girls around the house, through the side gate, and here to the porch. I went back inside briefly and grabbed these blankets for them.'

'Ok, thank you...Mr. Murphy.' He looked at Sophie.

'You are Sophie Dunover?'

'Yes sir.'

'Your date of birth?'

'March twenty-first, nineteen ninety two.'

'Social'

She gave it to him, providing a space between the digits. She felt Sarah shaking against her. She gave her a reassuring squeeze. She knew her part of the story would not be the same as Sarah's. She was in the basement for most of it. She had already worked out her story.

'Ok, so what happened here?'

I'm not completely certain. I was in the basement with Todd. We were, you know...she rolled her hands, hoping that he would get the idea without her actually having to say it. We got a little rough and the rack above us broke and came down all around us. A scythe hit him, and stuck in his head.' She stared at the floor, her eyes filling with water. She wiped at them. 'Before I came upstairs, I started to dress him. He didn't need to be naked when you guys showed up. I heard the back door slam after I got his pants on. That's when I went upstairs.'

'So, you were in the basement with Todd, having intercourse?'

'Yes sir. Sarah had gone upstairs to see what was going on. She said her boyfriend, Nate, had come to talk to her dad about something. She wanted to go find out what.'

'Why were you in the basement? Why did you stay there?'

'We went down because there was a box of stuff from her parents wedding. We were going to go through it and see what we could use for her wedding. I stayed because there was a table with some shackles attached to it. I thought it might be fun to have Todd come and we could "play around".

'Alright. So, when you came up from the basement...?'

When I came upstairs to find Sarah, because Todd was dead, she wasn't in her room, but Nate was dead in the hall upstairs. I went downstairs, to Mr. R's office. Her cell phone was broken in pieces near the wall on the other side of the room. When I went to pick it up, I saw Mr. R, dead under his desk. I walked around to his feet and found a gun.

'You found a gun? Do you know who it belonged to?'

'Yes sir. and no sir. I did not know who it belonged to.'

'Alright, continue.'

'Ok, so I picked up the gun and went through the house and saw Mrs. R. on the floor in the kitchen.'

'You picked up the gun?'

'Yes sir.'

'Why?'

'Protection sir.'

'What made you think you needed protection?'

'Latham what's his name, sir. I had to find Sarah, and there were two dead bodies. I knew he was dangerous, since he tried to rape me last night.'

'He tried to rape you? Last night?'

'Yes sir. We went out, Sarah and I, last night. No. Night before last. Sorry. She spent last night at my house. Anyway, Sarah had told me about him raping her, so we went out to clear her head. When we got back here, Mr. R demanded that I stay, as I had been drinking. Latham was there so I stayed in the guest house. He didn't care much for me so I figured he might show up, so I prepared for him. He did. I stabbed him in the arm when he attacked me.'

'I see. What happened next?' The officer nodded and did his best to poorly hide his smirk. He recalled his shift at the hospital night before last, when this guy came in saying he had been stabbed, and then told him he'd stabbed himself fixing a short in his truck. He knew it had been done by a woman.

'He left, bleeding all over the place. I don't know where he went after that.'

'Hospital.' Sarah volunteered.

The officer could barely contain his laughter. 'How do you know he went to the hospital?'

'Because he came in the next morning and raped me in my bedroom. Said I was paying for both of our behaviors. He was still wearing the wristband, and had a bandaid on his arm.'

'Alright. So you were in the basement, when the first gunshot went off?'

'No sir, I never heard the first gunshot.'

'It happened before she got here.'

Sophie looked hard at Sarah. That was not part of the story they had rehearsed. Concerned that Sarah was going to crack and tell them that she was going to confess to all of it, she rubbed her back. Nodding. 'I guess it happened before I got here."

Sarah stared at the ground. Her eyes wide and glossy. Her skin had lost its color, and she shivered. Shock was setting in. Sophie wrapped her tighter in her blanket. 'We should get her inside, sir. I think shock is setting in."

The officer shined his light on her face. 'I think you're right. Can she walk?' He spoke into his radio, calling for an ambulance to be sent immediately.

'Sarah, can you walk sweetie?'

Sarah didn't respond. She just stared at the ground.

'Sarah.' Sophie shook her gently.

Sarah looked at her. 'What?'

'Can you stand up, walk? We need to get you inside where it's warm.'

'I'm not cold.'

'I know you aren't. We don't want you to go into shock. Can you walk?"

'I think so.' She stood up. She wobbled and sat back down. It was harder for her to control her legs than she thought it would be. They felt like they were made of jelly. 'Maybe not.'

Sophie stood up and the officer stepped forward and helped her to her feet. She leaned hard on Sophie and let her help her into the house. She knew the rooms to avoid. She walked through the door and went to the left. She kept herself from looking in the study. She knew what was in there. She guided Sophie into the living room and plopped down in the middle of the couch.

Sophie took the blankets she was wrapped in and laid them over Sarah's front. She sat down next to Sarah and rubbed her back again.

'Ambulance is on its way. Can you go on?'

'Sure.' She kept her arms around Sarah.

'So, like I said, I found Mr. R and the gun. I went through the kitchen, found Mrs. R, and went out the back door.'

The officer interrupted. 'Was Mrs. R. dead or alive?'

'She was dead. A bloody mess.' She cringed. The image of Mrs. R. beaten to bloody death was terrible. The thought that it could have been Sarah...it made her skin crawl. Mrs. R wasn't the nicest lady, but she had no idea she was that bad. She stared at an imaginary spot on the wall.

'Ok, so you found Mrs. R. Did you touch her, move her at all?'

'No sir. I knew she was dead. So I went out back.'

'Alright. Then what?'

A third officer came through the front door and officer number two waved him in. 'Bus is here.'

'Alright, bring em in.'

'I don't want to go to the hospital.' Sarah gazed up into Sophie's eyes. The look on her face pleading with Sophie.

'It's ok honey. At least let them look you over. You took a pretty solid beating.'

'I'm fine. Really.'

The officer chimed in. 'We need to know you are alright, Ms. Rosenthal. You need to at least let them check you over. Make sure there is no internal bleeding or anything. Don't worry.' A smile stretched across his face.

Sarah's eyes shot to the officer. His face was round; a couple of chins skirted his neck. His eyes were a deep blue and showed signs of many sleepless nights. Even in his dark blue uniform, with a gun and a long flashlight, he didn't come across as threatening. Sarah relaxed some. 'Alright.' She leaned back on the couch and just rested.

The officer looked back at Sophie. 'Please continue.' He flipped the page on his note pad.

'So, I went out the back door and saw Sarah in the doorway of the guest house. Latham was in the chair. She flew backwards. I ran to the door. Latham was standing over her with a fireplace poker, about to smash it into her head. I shot him.'

'You shot him?'

'Yes sir. He was about to kill her. He was a monster. I knew that the night he came to get me in the guest house. He would have killed her.' She looked down at the floor.

'Anything else?'

'We sat there, on the floor, watching him. Making sure he wasn't going to get up again. Then DJ showed up. He brought us up here when we heard the sirens and we waited for you."

'Alright. Thank you Ms. Dunover.' He turned his attention to Sarah. 'Ms. Rosenthal, do you think you could tell me what happened from your perspective?'

Sarah didn't respond right away. Recalling the scene as they talked about it. Figuring out what she was going to say. 'They are all dead.' She really had not known what actually happened. She remembered hearing Nate in the study with her dad. Everything after that was really a blur.

She thought back. Nate and her dad were talking. She couldn't hear what they were saying. She shouldn't have been eavesdropping. She said it out loud. 'I shouldn't have been eavesdropping. He told me never to do it again. I did, and now they are all dead.'

'What do you mean?' The officer could see that she was distressed. He needed her statement, but in her current condition, she wouldn't be able to give anything helpful.

The paramedics moved into the room, carrying bags. In a flash they were on either side of Sarah, hooking her up to blood pressure cuffs, listening to her chest and her back. One of them worked on starting an IV while the other flashed a small pen light into each of her eyes and asked her questions.

'What's your name honey?'

'Sarah.'

'What day of the week is it?'

'Ummm, Sunday, I think.'

'Who is the president of the U.S?'

'Barack Obama.'

'Ok. What's your favorite sports team?'

'What? What kind of question is that right now?'

'It's one we ask to check your actual level of awareness. Worked huh?'

Sarah rolled her eyes. 'I'm fine. A few bumps and bruises, but I'm fine. He didn't get me this time.'

The lead paramedic looked at the officer. No signs of concussion or internal bleeding sir. She should be alright. Looks like the shock was from mental or emotional trauma, maybe? We have her on an IV to keep her hydrated, and can check her vitals for a while, but she seems to be ok.'

The officer nodded. 'Alright then. Can she talk?'

'I don't see why not. She answered my questions just fine.'

'Ok, thank you guys. Hang tight, over there in the corner for a bit, just to be certain, if you would?'

'Yes sir. We are running a heavy drip, she should be empty in about 15 minutes.' They picked up their bags and moved to the corner of the room by the entrance to the study.

Chapter 36

Just then, the first officer walked into the room. 'Just put the call in to the coroner. On the way. We have 5 bodies, four weapons have been recovered. A .38 caliber in the guest house, an umbrella, a scythe, and fireplace poker. Only two of the vics were shot. One was bludgeoned to death, one impaled with an umbrella in the abdomen, and one caught a scythe in the head, looks more accidental. The umbrella and the bludgeoning like they could go either way, the shooting in the study, hard to say since the firearm was moved.

Sophie stood up and turned to the first officer. 'I can show you where it was.' She looked back and forth between the two officers. "I am the one that moved it.'

The officers nodded at each other. The first officer stretched his arm out to her. 'Come on then.'

She took a few steps toward him and started to walk past him when he stopped her. 'Hold it. I need to check you for any other weapons.'

She stopped and turned around. Spread her legs and put her hands straight up in the air. 'I don't but go ahead."

The officer padded her down, asked her to turn around, and slid his hands from her shoulders to her waist, down the inside and outside of her legs and around each ankle. 'You're clean. Go on.'

She nodded and walked calmly into the study. She retraced her steps, walking to the wall, where pieces of Sarah's cell phone still lay on the floor. 'I came to the study, looked around the room and saw this. I recognized it as Sarah's and rushed to pick it up. As I bent down to pick it up, I saw something out of the corner of my eye. Mr. R, lying there staring at me. I stood up,' she stood up and walked toward the other side of the desk. 'I walked over here because there was a lot of blood on the floor near the top of his head. The gun was laying right there.' She pointed to the spot on the floor where the gun had been.

'Which way was it facing?'

She didn't even have to think about it. 'It was pointed toward the corner.' She pointed, indicating the corner of the room.

'Why did you pick it up?'

'I heard something. The door back door slammed. I didn't know if Latham had done this and was coming back or leaving. I didn't even know if it was loaded or not, just picked it up, hoping that it was, if just having it wasn't deterrent enough.'

'Who is Latham?'

'The dead guy in the guest house.'

'Did you shoot him?'

'Yes sir. I did.' She knew she was incriminating herself. It didn't matter though. He was about to kill Sarah. She had to shoot him. He was about to beat Sarah in the head with the fireplace poker.'

'Alright, let's go back and join the others.' He stretched his arm out again, allowing her to walk past him and out of the room. He walked over and placed a marker on the spot Sophie had pointed to and walked out of the room, joining her and the others.

'What is Latham's last name?' The first officer asked.

Sophie and DJ looked at each other and both shrugged their shoulders. 'We don't know.' Sophie said.

'Buchanan. His name was Latham Buchanan. He was my dad's associate, and tried to help my dad bury a secret.' A slight grin stretched her lips when the realization hit her that that was not the case anymore. She finally made up her mind. The asshole was going to take the wrap for all of this. She would see to it.

'A secret?' The second officer asked.

'Yes sir. A man, my actual father apparently, had come to blackmail him. He and my mom had an affair and conceived me. When she told him, he dumped her. He told this to my dad and he lost it. Choked the man nearly to death.'

'So, how were you involved in that?'

'I was snooping and saw it all. When Latham was carrying the man out to the guest house, we thought he was dead. Latham dragged me out there with him. He raped me, to keep me quiet.'

'So what happened to this guy? Your real father? Where is he now?'

'I really don't know. After I was raped, Latham had me wrap the guy up in a sheet and he left with him.'

'You have no idea where he took him?'

Sarah gave the officer a long hard look. 'Since he was alive, I figured he took him to the hospital and everything was fine. Then he followed me and raped me again, told me if I said a word about any of it that he would kill the guy and blame it on my dad. My dad didn't deserve that. So I kept quiet.'

'So what happened here then, tonight?'

The words flowed out of her like water. She knew exactly what happened. He killed them. He killed them all. 'I was at a party at Sophie's house, it was me and her, Todd and Nate. Nate and I were talking and had a fight. I left and came home. A few minutes later, while I was in my room, the doorbell rang. My dad answered it.'

'Where were you?'

'I was upstairs in my room. I'd come home and was changing into these ridiculously comfy pants. I loved these pants.' She looked down at the fuzzy blue pants with little rubber ducks on them, most of the yellow ducks were reddish orange now. Blood caked on them. Tears started to flow again.

'After I changed, I came downstairs to get something to drink and heard a voice that I recognized, but wasn't Latham's in my dad's study. The door was open a crack, so I peeked in.'

She fought to shut out the image that really happened. She changed it in her mind. Latham was there too, sitting in a chair across the room, but she hadn't seen him, as she and Sophie had discussed. 'I saw Nate sitting in the chair, my dad standing behind his desk. I couldn't hear what they were saying. It didn't look good though. My dad's face was all scrunched up.'

'How do you know Latham was in the room?'

'Because Nate turned around and looked at something behind him, jumped up out of the chair and put his hands up.'

'Ok, then what happened?'

'I saw something shiny move toward him. It took a second, but I realized it was a gun. I gasped and ran upstairs to my room. I hadn't gotten 3 steps when I heard the gun go off. I froze, right there in the hallway, and then ran again. Nate came up the stairs behind me. I heard Latham yelling behind him. They fought, right outside my bedroom door. I had locked it behind me and sat with my back against it until I heard footsteps go back down the stairs.'

She started to cry. The actual image of what happened. Nate running up the stairs behind her, thinking it was her father, and that he had killed Nate, grabbed the umbrella, shoved, spun around and saw Nate's eyes. Those beautiful blue eyes, filled with shock.

'Nate was bleeding. I rushed to him and pulled his head into my lap. He was bleeding badly. I started to go get a towel, but he asked me not to leave him. I stayed there, holding him. He died in my arms.' She sniffled and ran the blanket under her nose. She still stared blankly.

'Latham was at the bottom of the stairs, yelling at my mom. She was drunk, called him some bad names, and stumbled into the kitchen, still telling him he was stupid. I heard a strange pounding sound in the kitchen, so I ran down the stairs. He was sitting on top of her, pounding her head into the tile. I screamed and ran into the room. I pounded on his back, yelling at him to leave her alone. He stood up and reached for me. I ran out the back door and into the guest house before he could get a hold of me.'

She shifted in her seat. Seeing her mom there on the floor again in her mind. 'I grabbed the closest thing I could find and waited for him to come after me. When he stepped into the guest house, I swung the poker and caught him in the shoulder. We fought. I stabbed him in the chest with it and he fell back into the chair. He reached up and grabbed the poker with both hands and shoved toward me.

I fell backwards and landed on my butt. He stood up, pulled the poker out of his chest and lifted it over my head. He was going to bring it down on my head, but then there was a loud bang...he jerked strangely and he fell back into the chair. When I turned and looked where the bang came from, Sophie was standing in the doorway, the gun was still smoking.'

Chapter 37

Sophie is read her rights and placed in handcuffs. Sarah loses her shit. Tears are falling; screams are stuck in her throat and only come out as sobs. Sophie looks DJ in the eye, trying to communicate with him telepathically, hoping he understands what she wants.

He wraps his arms around Sarah, pulling her close to him. She buries her face in his chest. He whispers in her ear. 'Shhh shh shh sweetie. It's gonna be ok. We will get her out. This is the legal process. She can't just walk away. It will be alright.' He smoothed her hair, holding her tightly while she sobbed.

Sarah didn't think she could cry anymore. She was dead tired and didn't want to answer any more questions, be examined any more, and she definitely didn't want to be here, while they carried the bodies out. 'Can we get out of here? I can't deal with this anymore right now.'

'I understand. Let's find out.' He rubbed her back and eased his hold on her, making sure she was stable on her feet before he completely let go. He walked over to the 2nd officer and they spoke quietly. The officer looked over at Sarah and nodded. She saw his mouth move but didn't make out what he was saying.

DJ walked back over to her and put his arm back around her. 'He says we can go. He has our information, not to leave the state, blah blah blah. Do you need to grab some things before we go?'

'Yeah, will you come upstairs with me, just to the door. I don't want to be up there alone...with Nate.'

'Sure, sure. Let's go.' He turned with his arm still around her. They went up the stairs. An officer was perched at the top of the stairs. A sheet had been draped over Nate's body. She was grateful for that. She went into her room, DJ turned his back at the door and stood facing the officer until she returned.

Sarah stripped out of her bloody clothes. She dropped them in a pile near the door. She grabbed the backpack she had taken with her to Sophie's. The clothes in it were still clean. She pulled out a few other outfits and stuffed them in the backpack. She went to the closet and pulled out a large duffle bag. She went into her bathroom and gathered up several items. She anticipated not coming back here for a while. She pulled items out of each drawer.

She closed the back pack and zipped the duffle and threw one over each shoulder. She went to the door and tapped DJ gently on the shoulder. He stepped aside, turned to face her, and took the duffle from her. She stepped back into the room and grabbed her purse.

They went back downstairs. She went to the closet under the stairs and pulled out three different jackets. She put the heaviest, a soft black leather that stopped just below her knees, on and stuck the other two under her arm. She walked over to the table next to the front door and picked up her keys.

They went out the front door and she headed toward her car. She opened the back door and threw the backpack in. It landed in the middle of the back seat. She turned around to take the duffle from DJ. She looked across the street to the big brown truck parked there.

'DJ, I don't think I can drive.'

'It's ok. I'll drive you. I can get a ride tomorrow back over here to get the truck and head in to the shop from here. Don't worry.'

She handed him the keys and dragged herself around to the passenger side of her car. The second officer walked out and moved his vehicle into the driveway. He got out and walked over to Sarah. 'How do we reach you if we have any other questions and how should we lock up when we are done here?'

'There is another set of keys on the table in there. Use them to lock up. As for how to reach me...DJ? My phone was destroyed.'

'Call me. She'll be at my place as long as she needs to be. If you would, See that Sophie gets my number also. She will need it.'

'Sure thing, sir. You guys try to have a better night.'

Sarah nodded and fell into the passenger seat of her car. The officer checked for fingers and toes and pushed her door shut. DJ slid into the driver's seat and pulled his door shut. 'Are you ready?'

'Yeah, please get me the fuck out of here.'

DJ started the car, put it in reverse, and backed slowly out of the driveway. He drove the speed limit. They had been in the car together for almost ten minutes before either of them spoke. DJ finally broke the silence. 'Are you alright?"

'No.' She answered simply enough. 'My family and the man I wanted to marry are gone. Just like that. Gone. My best friend has been taken to jail for no reason, and I'm letting an almost complete stranger drive my car to I have no idea where. I don't know what alright is right now.'

'I can accept that. I know it has to be a lot to deal with right now. I'm not a complete stranger though. I've known you for years now little lady.'

'I said almost complete. You have been coming to my house almost every day since forever. I don't know anything about you though. Other than you drive that big brown truck and deliver packages. I actually feel a little bad about it.'

DJ laughed out loud. 'There isn't much else to know. I work about eighteen hours a day, delivering packages. I go home and sleep at the end of the day, get up the next morning and do it all over again. I only work half days on Saturdays and on Sundays, I usually hang around the house in my boxers, watching a game or something.'

'Wow.' She snickered. 'That really is about all, huh?"

'Sarah, I gotta tell you. I'm soo sorry I didn't notice that something might be off with you and your family. If I had known...'

'Don't worry about that DJ. It was my fault. If I had spoken up, things would have ended a lot differently, but none of it would have ended well for me or my dad. It's all my fault.'

'Shhh. Don't even think about that right now. We need to keep you calm and relaxed.'

'I can't be calm and relaxed. My whole family is gone and it's all my fault. They might have bought the story tonight, but eventually, it's all going to come out.'

'We will cross that bridge when we get to it. For now, the only thing you need to worry about is what you want to eat tonight...and tomorrow. I'm a single guy, live alone, and the contents of my fridge leave a lot to be desired.'

'Oh geez, I don't think I'll be able to eat for a while. Don't worry about that.'

'Bullshit. You have to eat to keep your strength up. I'm not taking no for an answer, so you decide what you want or I'll just get something for you and you will have to eat it.'

Her head snapped to her left. 'Seriously?'

'You gotta eat. I'm not gonna sit on you and force it down your throat, but I promised Sophie I would take care of you, so you gotta eat, or I've let her down.'

'Oh. Well I suppose that makes sense. I don't know what I could eat right now. I really don't. What I want right now, is a scalding hot shower and a very long nap. I might be able to eat a sandwich or something tomorrow. I can go out and get it tomorrow though.'

Well, I can take you to the house, you can get a shower while I go out and get something, then, when I get back, we can see how you feel about eating then, or we can just get you tucked in to bed. How does that sound?'

'That sounds like a plan. Thank you for understanding.'

'Don't mention it.'

Chapter 38

They drove along in silence for about another ten minutes when he pulled into a short driveway that ran between two houses. He put the car into park. 'Here we are. Home sweet home.'

She looked at her surroundings. It was dark, so there wasn't a lot of visible detail she could see, but she got a comfortable vibe from the area. She opened her door and stepped out. She opened the back door and dragged her back pack across the seat and threw it over her shoulder.

DJ opened up the back door and pulled out her duffle bag, threw it over his shoulder and closed the door. He walked around the car, put his arm around Sarah, closed the car door, and led her to the front porch.

He fumbled around in his pocket for his house key. He pulled it out, placed it in the lock and shook it, stopped and shook it again, stopped and shook it one more time, in a kind of code. He looked at her and smiled. She didn't catch the reference. He rolled his eyes. 'Remind me to educate you on the finer points of Pet Detective later.'

'Shit, I'm sorry. That should have been funny. I've seen the movie, and I loved it. I'm just not paying attention right now. I'm sorry.'

'Don't worry about it. It was cheesy anyway.' He turned the key in the lock and opened the door. He stepped back out of the doorway and stretched his arm out to allow her to enter first.

She stepped inside a few feet. It was very dark. Her skin crawled. Something didn't feel right. The light clicked on, blinding her for a second. When she saw the quaintly decorated living room, with no one but her in it, she relaxed a little.

She was in a stranger's house. Sure, she knew DJ enough to point him out in a crowd, and tell someone what he did for a living, but other than that, she knew nothing. He now knew her though. Her darkest secrets had been laid out to him in a matter of moments.

At that moment, she was glad he had shown up. He had helped her keep her story straight, kept a handle on her when they took Sophie away, and had gotten her away from the house. She appreciated him for all of it. Something wasn't right about it though.

DJ came in behind her, closed the door, and gestured for her to follow him. She nodded and followed him to the first door on the left down a little hallway. He reached into the room, found the switch, and the room lit up.

It was empty of all but a bed. 'I'll go get the makings while you settle in.' He walked in and set her bag on the floor next to the bed then he was gone. She stepped into the room and felt instantly uncomfortable again. The hair on the back of her neck stood on end and red flags flapped a mile a minute in her mind's eye. She had to get out of the room.

She heard DJ's phone ring as she headed back down the hallway. She stopped in the middle of the living room, between the couch and the fireplace. It really was a quaint little place and she struggled to figure out why she felt so uncomfortable.

That's when she saw it. There on the mantle, right in the middle, a wooden frame surrounded a photograph. It was the man that her dad had killed, younger and with a woman about his same age. Right smack between them was DJ. He was just a little boy, but it was obviously him.

Panic took over her. She started to shake. She backed away from the fireplace as DJ came flying into the room. He stopped directly in front of her and reached to put his arms around her, yelling. 'They found him! He's alive and at Latham's...' The realization struck him like a brick. Rage flashed in his eyes as it all came together for him in a split second.

His father had been missing for over a week now. Sarah's dad tried to kill him and Latham was holding him hostage. Sarah knew about it. He glared at her. Wrapping his hands hard around her arms, he shook her. 'You knew!'

She didn't know what to say. She had just realized herself who the man was. If she had known who it was, she would have told him, she was sure of it. Panic took over though. He was angry. She recognized the look in his eyes. She raised her arms and shoved DJ backwards.

The force of her shove knocked them both backwards. She landed sitting on the couch. DJ wasn't so lucky.

He fell backwards, hitting the back of his head hard on the mantle and fell to the floor. Small flecks of blood spattered into the fireplace and across the wall as his head bounced once and then flipped to the right. Thick red blood pooled out beneath his head. His eyes still angry, stared at the wall.

Sarah impacted with the couch just a split second before DJ hit the floor. She watched him fall in slow motion. When she saw his head bounce off the floor and blood fly, she jumped up darted toward the front door.

She collided with the door and struggled with the knob,

screaming and sobbing. It finally opened, and she flung it back, nearly taking her own arm off at the elbow as she whipped around it to get out.

She stumbled out into the porch, her legs trembling like they were made of jello, refused to support her weight another second. In a single instant and a final step, her knees buckled, toppling her to the floor like a tower of blocks.

Her shoulder slammed down hard on the concrete at the very edge of the porch. Her head rolled downward and stopped, with a snap, against the top step. She took a breath, seeing flashes of her life playing like a movie in fast forward. Latham, slumped and bloody in the chair in the guest house was the last thing she saw. A smile stretched across her face as she exhaled, and her world went dark.

The End

About the Author

Christy spends the better part of her days staring at her laptop screen, waiting for her muse to divulge the secrets of new dark fiction and non-fiction and working heavily on self-improvement. When not being tortured by said muse and meditating she spends her time helping others write, publish, and market their books, either through her publishing company, Twisted Souls Press or her Save Your Sanity Publishing Assistance service.

Follow Christy on her website, facebook and twitter
https://christymannauthor.com